Minor Key

For Jim Burns
writer, editor, jazz aficionado...
a little older and much the wiser

Minor Key

www.fiveleaves.co.uk

Minor Key
by John Harvey

Published in 2009 by Five Leaves,
PO Box 8786, Nottingham NG1 9AW
www.fiveleaves.co.uk

ISBN: 978 1 905512 73 7

Minor Key is printed in a limited edition of 500,
with all copies signed by the author

John Harvey's website is www.mellotone.co.uk

All author royalties from this book are being donated to The
Place2Be, specifically for the work it is doing to help foster the
emotional development of children in Nottingham Primary Schools.
www.theplace2be.org.uk

Five Leaves acknowledges financial support from
Arts Council England

Five Leaves is a member of Inpress
(www.inpressbooks.co.uk)
representing independent publishers.

Cover design: Darius Hinks
Typeset and design: Four Sheets Design and Print
Printed in Great Britain

Contents

Resnick, Nottingham and All That Jazz

"Write about what you know," used to be — possibly still is — one of the first precepts passed on to would-be writers. As a piece of advice it's always struck me as limited — whither imagination? — and, as someone who has latterly made something of a career out of criminal acts ranging from petty larceny to murder, not one that, if adhered to, would have done me a great deal of good. My first book, after all, *Avenging Angel*, published by New English Library in 1975 under the name of Thom Ryder, didn't shy away from detailing the lives of a gang of dangerous Hell's Angels, despite my knowledge of bikers extending no further than the brief ownership of a Honda 50. Nor did never having fired a handgun or having only once ridden a horse prevent me from writing somewhere between forty and fifty westerns.

Just about the best advice I've read about learning to write comes in Stephen King's excellent little book, *On Writing; A Memoir of the Craft* — "If you want to be a writer, you must do two things above all others: read a lot and write a lot." Obvious? You would think so. Too obvious to be worth saying? Ask anyone who's tried to teach creative writing.

Maybe there are some writers who arrive at the keyboard fully-fledged, fully-formed, just as there are some thirteen year olds who breeze through mathematics at Oxford with flying colours; but for the rest of us, most of us, there's no avoiding putting in the effort, putting in the hours. As King says, "There's no way around these two things that I'm aware of, no shortcut."

I guess the only thing I might add, referring back to the beginning, is that it helps to know something.

Before I wrote my first crime novels in the mid-70s, the deservedly short-lived Scott Mitchell series, I'd done my background reading — Chandler, Hammett, Ross Macdonald, George V. Higgins, early Robert Parker, Ed McBain — learned the basic moves, and had come up with a reasonably attractive, if somewhat self-pitying, private eye, but, although the books were ostensibly set in England, my hero remained resolutely stranded somewhere over the mid-Atlantic: no grit, no traction, no sense of place.

That didn't really come until I was involved in a television series about the probation service, the officers and their clients, called *Hard Cases*. Although some of the interiors were filmed in the old Central Television studios off Clifton Boulevard in Nottingham, much of it was shot on location in the city and it was this, I think, along with the experience of juggling the various strands of narrative the programme demanded, that turned me towards the idea of writing a crime novel with a specific Nottingham setting. By then I'd lived there, in two spells, getting on for fifteen years and it felt at least as much like home as the patch of north London where I grew up. Working on the TV scripts, I'd developed a routine: write early, walk into the centre from Lenton, have coffee at the stall in the Victoria Centre market, walk back, write some more. Other times, I caught the bus, ears open, wandered around, avidly read the *Post,* listened to local radio, stood on the terraces at Meadow

Lane. I was not a native and, especially now I've retreated back to London, never will be, but I did feel I knew enough to set a book believably in the city.

When I was coming up with the idea of Resnick, beginning to see him in my mind, it helped being able to picture him walking down a specific street, the Alfreton Road, say, or crossing the Old Market Square; when I was writing, it helped to know where exactly he would come to if he turned left, if he turned right. Though he was never me, he went to some of the same places I did; listened to lunchtime jazz, for instance, in The Bell, shared my seat at the espresso stall, had a pint and a cheese and onion cob in the Peacock (renamed, for some reason I don't remember, the Partridge) cheered on Tommy Johnson and Rachid Harkouk at Meadow Lane, remembered drinking at the Black Boy and the Flying Horse.

It was regularly walking past the group of Poles who used to congregate in the Victoria Centre, outside the entrance to the market, that put it into my mind that Resnick might be from a Polish background, his family having migrated here during World War Two. I liked the idea that he was of the city and yet not of the city — a bit like myself, in fact — that he belonged, yet didn't belong, an insider with an outsider's eye. (The Detective as Writer, discuss.)

And when I began writing the first books, Nottingham was in a process of change; some of the bigger industries — Raleigh, Players — were still major employers, part of the city's fabric. Beneath an ostensibly benign surface, the gap between comparatively rich and poor was widening and has continued to do so and, because the city is relatively small, this was and is all too evident. I'd lived in Lenton and lived in the Park, my son lives in St. Ann's; I know what it's like south of the Trent in the comfortable suburbs of West Bridgford and Edwalton, just beyond the city's boundaries, and I know that the constituency of

Nottingham North has the highest rate of teenage pregnancy in Western Europe and sends fewer people on to university than any other area in Britain.

Those contrasts make the city a fertile place about which to write and, often sadly, bring with them ready grist to the crime writer's mill.

But now, jazz.

Why jazz?

On the one hand, it's part of fleshing Resnick out with a few characteristics which suggest appetite, an inner life, imagination; on the other, it goes back to what I was saying about bringing to the work a little of something you know.

For me, jazz, like so many things, started at secondary school. I remember being in the playground one day with a copy of the *NME* and being accosted by one of the older boys and told, "You don't want to be reading that. That's all pop rubbish. You want to read the *Melody Maker* — that's where the jazz is." (Those *were* the days.)

Jazz was cool.

Jazz was what the kids who sneaked off down to the Archway to hang out and smoke cigarettes were listening to.

Jazz was a series of clubs all over north London — Finchley and Barnet and Wood Green — or, for the more daring, it was Soho and jiving at Humph's in Oxford Street, or bedding down on the floor of Studio 51 beneath duffle coats after a Ken Colyer all-nighter, then frothy coffee in a glass cup at Sam Widges or the Bar Italia before, spent up, walking home.

That I spread my wings beyond homegrown trad and Dixieland — and, gradually, blues and skiffle — was as much as anything due to an uncle of one of my school friends, whose collection of vinyl 78s we were allowed to pick through, and which included Ellington and Earl Bostic and Louis Jordan's Tympany Five — and Billie Holiday. The first song of hers I ever heard: "I Cried for You" by Teddy Wilson and his Orchestra, with Billie Holiday, vocal refrain. It was a good while later that I discovered the alto sax on that record was played by Johnny Hodges, or that the trumpet player on "Billie's Blues", another of the 78s laying around, was Bunny Berigan.

It was an experience of getting to know the music that I borrowed and recast for Charlie Resnick in the third of the novels, *Cutting Edge*.

> *Resnick had sat in silence with black tea and dry cake while his uncle handsewed buttonholes and hems and his cousin swayed her legs softly to the Ink Spots, the Mills Brothers, four voices and a guitar.*
>
> *After a while, his uncle would tap his thimble on the table and wink at Resnick and then they would listen to Mildred Bailey, Billie Holiday, Luis Russell's "Call of the Freaks", Fats Waller and his Rhythm, "The Joint is Jumpin'".*

I've carried on listening to jazz and so has Charlie, though our tastes remain pretty much where they were formed, the music of the forties and fifties and early sixties, mainstream and swing shading into bop. One thing that he and I share, aside from watching Notts County whenever the opportunity arises: not many days go by without our listening to Thelonius Monk.

What I've tried to suggest with Resnick is that there's some kind of subliminal link between the feelings engendered by the music he listens to and his understanding of the emotions of others, the victims and sometimes the perpetrators he encounters in his daily life and work, the things they feel and do. And I've done my best, here and there, to describe what he hears, how it sounds, this jazz, the joy and the sadness it can bring.

So this little book from Nottingham's Five Leaves tips a hat towards Charlie and the city in which he fictionally thrives, just as it taps its feet to a walking bass and a regular four-four rhythm. It acknowledges, in its quiet way, that, by virtue of good friends and good fortune and always remembering to look right, left and right again, I'm now safely embarked on my seventh decade, leaving some 100 published books in my wake — this, if I've counted correctly, being number 101.

The first story in the collection, and the only one not to have Resnick present, is "Minor Key", which had its beginnings in the Soho I've alluded to above and then moves to Paris, following its central character, the mixed-race saxophone player, Valentine Collins, as he seeks to leave various of his troubles behind. It's one of several short stories I've written involving the same quartet of characters — Val, Jimmy, Patrick and Anna — as a way of testing the ground for that novel set in and around the jazz and club world of Soho in the 50s, 60s and onwards — the one Jim Burns is anxious to help me research and which neither my editor nor my agent think I'm ever actually going to write.

The other stories are set in Nottingham and, in addition to Resnick, find room on a couple of occasions for Lynn Kellogg, whose career in the police force has progressed in accordance with her abilities, and whose relationship with Charlie has also moved on, so that, by the date of the later stories here, they are contentedly living together. Eileen Cook, previously in at least one novel and several short stories, reappears in both "Billie's Blues" and "The Sun, the Moon and the Stars", and, survivor that she is, I wouldn't take bets on her not turning up again.

Minor Key

It used to be there under Birthdays, some years at least. The daily listing in the paper, the *Guardian*, occasionally the *Times*. September 18th. Valentine Collins, jazz musician. And then his age: 27, 35, 39. Not 40. Val never reached 40.

He'd always look, Val, after the first time he was mentioned, made a point of it, checking to see if his name was there. "Never know," he'd say, with that soft smile of his — "Never know if I'm meant to be alive or dead."

There were times when we all wondered; wondered what it was going to be. Times when he seemed to be chasing death so hard, he had to catch up. Times when he didn't care.

Jimmy rang me this morning, not long after I'd got back from the shops. Bread, milk, eggs — the paper — gives me something to do, a little walk, reason to stretch my legs.

"You all right?" he says.

"Of course I'm all right."

"You know what day it is?"

I hold my breath; there's no point in shouting, losing my temper. "Yes, Jimmy, I know what day it is."

There's a silence and I can sense him reaching for the words, the thing to say — You don't fancy meeting up later? A drink, maybe? Nice to have a chat. It's been a while.

"Okay, then, Anna," he says instead, and then he hangs up.

There was a time when we were inseparable, Jimmy, Val, Patrick and myself. Studio 51, the Downbeat Club, all-nighters at the Flamingo, coffee at the Bar Italia, spaghetti at the Amalfi. That place on Wardour Street where Patrick swore the cheese omelettes were the best he'd ever tasted and Val would always punch the same two buttons on the juke box, B19 and 20, both sides of Ella Fitzgerald's single, "Manhattan" and "Every Time We Say Goodbye".

Val loved that song, especially.

He knew about goodbyes, Val.

Later, anyway.

Back then it was just another sad song, something to still the laughter. Which is what I remember most from those years, the laughter. The four of us marching arm in arm through the middle of Soho, carefree, laughing.

What do they call them? The fifties? The years of austerity? That's not how I remember them, 56, 57, 58. Dancing, music and fun, that's what they were to me. But then, maybe I was too young, too unobservant, too — God! It seems impossible to believe or say — but, yes, too innocent to know what was already there, beneath the surface. Too stupid to read the signs.

Patrick, for instance, turning away from the rest of us to have quick, intense conversations in corners with strangers, men in sharp suits and sharp haircuts, Crombie overcoats. The time Patrick himself suddenly arrived one evening in a spanking new three piece suit from Cecil Gee, white shirt with a rolled Mr B. collar, soft Italian shoes, and when we asked him where the cash came for all that, only winking and tapping the side of his nose with his index finger — mind yours.

Val, those moments when he'd go quiet and stare off into nowhere and you knew, without anyone saying, that you couldn't speak to him, couldn't touch him, just had to leave him be until he'd turn, almost shyly, and smile with his eyes.

And Jimmy, the way he'd look at me when he thought no one else was noticing; how he couldn't bring himself to say the right words to me, even then.

And if I had seen them, the signs of our future, would it have made any difference, I wonder? Or would it all have turned out the same? Sometimes you only see what you want to until something presses your face so fast up against it there's nothing else you can do.

But in the beginning it was the boys and myself and none of us with a care in the world. Patrick and Jimmy had known one another since they were little kids at primary school, altar boys together at St. Pat's; Val had met up with them later, the second year of the grammar school — and me, I'd been lucky enough to live in the same street, catch the same bus in the morning, lucky enough that Jimmy's mother and mine should be friends. The boys were into jazz, jazz and football — though for Patrick it was the Arsenal and Jimmy, Spurs, and the rows they had about that down the years. Val now, in truth I don't think Val ever cared too much about the football, just went along, White Hart Lane or Highbury, he didn't mind.

When it came to jazz, though, it was Val who took the lead, and where the others would have been happy enough to listen to anything as long as it had rhythm, excitement, as long as it had swing, Val was the one who sat them down and made them listen to Gerry Mulligan with Chet Baker, Desmond with Brubeck, Charlie Parker, Lester Young.

With a few other kids they knew, they made themselves into a band: Patrick on trumpet, Jimmy on drums, Val with an ageing alto saxophone that had belonged to his dad. After the first couple of rehearsals it became clear Val was the only one who could really play. I mean really play: the kind of sound that gives you goose bumps on the arms and makes the muscles of your stomach tighten hard.

It wasn't long before Patrick had seen the writing on the wall and turned in his trumpet in favour of becoming agent and manager rolled into one; about the first thing he did was sack Jimmy from the band, Val's was the career to foster and Jimmy was just holding him back.

A couple of years later, Val had moved on from sitting in with Jackie Sharpe and Tubby Hayes at the Manor House, and depping with Oscar Rabin's band at the Lyceum, to fronting a quartet that slipped into the lower reaches of the Melody Maker small group poll. Val was burning the proverbial candle, going on from his regular gig to some club where he'd play till the early hours and taking more Bennies than was prudent to keep himself awake. The result was, more than once, he showed up late for an engagement; occasionally, he didn't show up at all. Patrick gave him warning after warning, Val, in return, made promises he couldn't keep: in the end, Patrick, delivered an ultimatum, finally walked away.

Within months the quartet broke up and, needing ready cash, Val took a job with Lou Preager's Orchestra back at the Lyceum: a musical diet that didn't stretch far beyond playing for dancers, the occasional novelty number and the hits of the day. At least when he'd been with Rabin there'd been a few other jazzers in the band — and Oscar had allowed them one number a night to stretch out and do their thing. But this ... the boredom, the routine were killing him, and Val, I realised later, had moved swiftly on from chewing the insides of Benzedrine inhalers and smoking cannabis to injecting heroin. When the police raided a club in Old Compton Street in the small hours, there was Val in a back room with a needle in his arm.

Somehow, Patrick knew one of the detectives at West End

Central well enough to call in a grudging favour. Grudging, but a favour all the same.

When Val stumbled out on to the pavement, twenty-four hours later and still wearing the clothes he'd puked up on, Patrick pushed him into a cab and took him to the place I was living in Kilburn.

I made tea, poured Patrick the last of a half bottle of whisky, and ran a bath for Val, who was sitting on the side of my bed in his vest and underpants, shivering.

"You're a stupid bastard. You know that, don't you?" Patrick told him.

Val said nothing.

"He's a musician, I told the copper," Patrick said. "A good one. And you know what he said to me? All he is, another black junkie out of his fucking head on smack. Send him back where he fucking came from."

A shadow of pain passed across Val's face and I looked away, ashamed, not knowing what to say. Val's father was West Indian, his mother Irish, his skin the colour of palest chocolate.

"Can you imagine?" Patrick said, turning to me. "All those years and I never noticed." Reaching out, he took hold of Val's jaw and twisted his face upwards towards the light. "Look at that. Black as the ace of fucking spades. Not one of us at all."

"Stop it," I said. "Stop it, for God's sake. What's the matter with you?"

Patrick loosed his hold and stepped away. "Trying to shake some sense into him. Make him realise, way he's going, what'll happen if he carries on."

He moved closer to Val and spoke softly. "They've got your number now, you know that, don't you? Next time they catch you with as much as smelling of reefer they're going to have you inside so fast your feet won't touch the ground. And you won't like it inside, believe me."

Val closed his eyes.

"What you need is to put a little space between you and them, give them time to forget." Patrick stepped back. "Give me a couple of days, I'll sort something. Even if it's the Isle of Man."

In the event, it was Paris. A two-week engagement at *Le Chat Qui Peche* with an option to extend it by three more.

"You better go with him, Anna. Hold his hand, keep him out of trouble." And slipping an envelope fat with French francs and two sets of tickets into my hand, he kissed me on the cheek. "Just his hand, mind."

The club was on the rue de la Huchette, close to the Seine, a black metal cat perched above a silver-grey fish on the sign outside; downstairs a small, smoky cellar bar with a stage barely big enough for piano, bass and drums, and, for seating, perhaps the most uncomfortable stools I've ever known. Instruments of torture, someone called them and, by the end of the first week, I knew exactly what he meant.

Not surprisingly, the French trio with whom Val was due to work were suspicious of him at first. His reputation in England may have been on the rise, but across the Channel he was scarcely known. And when you're used to visitors of the calibre of Miles Davis and Bud Powell, Charlie Parker, what gave Val Collins the idea he'd be welcome? Didn't the French have saxophone players of their own?

Both the bassist and the drummer wore white shirts that first evening, I remember, ties loosened, top buttons undone, very cool; the pianist's dark jacket was rucked up at the back, its collar arched awkwardly against his neck, a cigarette smouldering, half-forgotten, at the piano's edge.

The proprietor, Madame Ricard, welcomed us with lavish kisses and led us to a table, where we sat listening, the club not yet half full, Val's foot moving instinctively to the rhythm and his fingers flexing over imaginary keys. At the intermission, she introduced us to the band, who shook hands politely, looked at Val with cursory interest and excused themselves to stretch their legs outside, breath in a little night air.

"Nice guys," Val said with a slight edge as they left.

"You'll be fine," I said and squeezed his arm.

When the trio returned, Val was already on stage, re-angling the mike, adjusting his reed. "Blues in F," he said quietly, counting in the tempo, medium-fast. After a single chorus from the piano, he announced himself with a squawk and then a skittering run and they were away. Ten minutes later, when Val stepped back from the microphone, layered in sweat, the drummer gave a little triumphant roll on his snare, the pianist turned and held out his hand and the bass player loosened another button on his shirt and grinned.

"*Et maintenant*," Val announced, testing his tender vocabulary to the full, "*nous jouons une ballade par Ira Gershwin et Vernon Duke*, 'I Can't Get Started.' *Merci.*"

And the crowd, accepting him, applauded.

What could go wrong?

At first, nothing it seemed. We both slept late most days at the hotel on the rue Maitre-Albert where we stayed; adjacent rooms that held a bed, a small wardrobe and little else, but with views across towards Notre Dame. After coffee and croissants — we were in Paris, after all — we would wander around the city, the streets of Saint-Germain-des-Prés at first, but then, gradually, we found our way around Montparnasse and up through Montmartre to Sacre Coeur. Sometimes we would take in a late afternoon movie, and Val would have a nap at the hotel before a leisurely dinner and on to the club for that evening's session, which would continue until the early hours.

Six nights a week and on the seventh, rest?

There were other clubs to visit, other musicians to hear. The Caveau de la Huchette was just across the street, the Club Saint-Germain-des-Prés and the Trois Mailletz both a short walk away. Others, like the Tabou and the Blue Note were a little further afield. I couldn't keep up.

"Go back to the hotel," Val said, reading the tiredness in my eyes. "Get a good night's sleep, a proper rest." Then, with the beginnings of a smile, "You don't have to play nursemaid all the time, you know."

"Is that what I'm doing?"

Coming into the club late one evening, I saw him in the company of an American drummer we'd met a few nights before and a couple of broad-shouldered French types, wearing those belted trench coats which made them look like cops or gangsters or maybe both. As soon as he spotted me, Val made a quick show of shaking hands and turning away, but not before I saw a small package pass from hand to hand and into the inside pocket of his suit.

"Don't look so disapproving," he said, when I walked over. "Just a few pills to keep me awake."

"And that's all?"

"Of course." He had a lovely, disarming smile.

"No smack?"

"No smack."

I could have asked him to show me his arms, but I chose to believe him instead. It would have made little difference if I had; by then I think he was injecting himself in the leg.

The next day Val was up before eleven, dressed and ready, stirring me from sleep.

"What's happening?" I asked. "What's wrong?"

"Nothing. Just a shame to waste a beautiful day."

The winter sun reflected from the stonework of the bridge as we walked across to the Isle St. Louis arm in arm. Val had taken to affecting a beret, which he wore slanting extravagantly to one side. On the cobbles close to where we sat, drinking coffee, sparrows splashed in the shallow puddles left by last night's rain.

"Why did you do it?" Val asked me.

"Do it?"

"This. All of this. Throwing up your job..."

"It wasn't a real job."

"It was work."

"It was temping in a lousy office for a lousy boss."

"And this is better?"

"Of course this is better."

"I still don't understand why?"

"Why come here with you?"

Val nodded.

"Because he asked me."

"Patrick."

"Yes, Patrick."

"You do everything he asks you?"

I shook my head. "No. No, I don't."

"You will," he said. "You will." I couldn't see his eyes; I didn't want to see his eyes.

A foursome of tourists, Scandinavian I think, possibly German, came and sat noisily at a table nearby. When the waiter walked past, Val asked for a cognac, which he poured into what was left of his coffee and downed at a single gulp.

"What I meant," he said, "would you have come if it had been anyone else but me?"

"I know what you meant," I said. "And, no. No, I don't think I would."

"Jimmy, perhaps?"

"Yes," I acknowledged. "Perhaps Jimmy. Maybe."

Seeing Val's rueful smile, I reached across and took hold of his hand, but when, a few moments later, he gently squeezed my fingers, I took my hand away.

Patrick was waiting for us at the hotel when we returned.

"Well," he said, rising from the lobby's solitary chair. "The lovebirds at last."

"Bollocks," Val said, but with a grin.

Patrick kissed the side of my mouth and I could smell tobacco and scotch and expensive aftershave; he put his arms round Val and gave him a quick hug.

"Been out for lunch?"

"Breakfast," Val said.

"Fine. Then let's have lunch."

Over our protests he led us a small restaurant in the Latin Quarter, where he ordered in a combination of enthusiastic gestures and sixth form French.

"I went along to the club earlier," Patrick said, once the waiter had set a basket of bread on the table and poured our wine. "Sounds as if it's going well. Madame Ricard wants to hold you over for three weeks more. Assuming you're agreeable?"

Val nodded. "Sure."

"Anna?"

"I can't stay that long," I said.

"Why ever not?" Patrick looked surprised, aggrieved.

"I've got a life to live."

"You've got a bedsit in Kilburn and precious little else."

Blood rushed to my cheeks. "All the more reason, then, for not wasting my time here."

Patrick laughed. "You hear that, Val? Wasting her time."

"Let her be," Val said, forcefully.

Patrick laughed again. "Found yourself a champion," he said, looking at me.

Val's knife struck the edge of his plate. "For fuck's sake!

When are you going to stop organising our lives?"

Patrick took his time in answering. "When I think you can do it for yourselves."

In his first set that evening, Val was a little below par, nothing most of the audience seemed to notice or be bothered by, but there was less drive than usual to his playing and several of his solos seemed to peter out aimlessly before handing over to the piano. I could sense the tension building in Patrick beside me, and after the third number he steered me outside; there was a faint rain misting across the headlights of the cars along the Quai Saint-Michel and from the bridge leading across to the Île de la Cité, the river water looked black and unforgiving.

"He's using again," Patrick said. "You know that, don't you?"

I shook my head. "I don't think so."

"Anna, come on…"

"I asked him."

"You asked him and he said no?"

"Yes."

"Scout's honour, cross my heart and hope to die. That kind of no?"

I pulled away from him. "Don't do that."

"Do what?"

"Treat me as though I'm some child."

"Then open your eyes."

"They are open."

Patrick sighed and I saw the grey of his breath dissembling into the night air.

"I'm not his jailer, Patrick," I said. "I'm not his wife, his lover. I can't watch him twenty-four hours of the day."

"I know."

He kissed me on the forehead, the sort of kiss you might give to a young girl, his lips cold and quick. A long, low boat passed slowly beneath the bridge.

23

"I'm opening a club," he said. "Soho. Broadwick Street."

"You?"

"Some friends I know, they're putting up the money. I thought if Val were interested it would be somewhere for him to play."

"What about the police? Isn't that a risk still?"

Patrick smiled. "Don't worry about that. It's all squared away."

How many times would I hear him say that over the years? All squared away. How much cash was shelled out, usually in small denominations, unmarked notes slipped into side pockets or left in grubby holdalls in the left-luggage lockers of suburban railway stations? I never knew the half of it, the paybacks and back handers and all the false accounting, not even during those years later when we lived together — another story, waiting, one day, to be told.

"Come on," he said, taking my arm. "We'll miss the second set."

When we got back to the club, Val and the American drummer were in animated conversation at the far end of the bar. Seeing us approach, the drummer ducked his head towards Val, spoke quickly and stepped away. "It's not me you have to worry about, you fucker, remember that." And then he was pushing his way through the crowd.

"What was all that about?" Patrick asked.

Val shrugged. "Nothing. Why?"

"He seemed pretty angry."

"It doesn't mean anything. That's just the way he is."

"How much do you owe?"

"What?"

"That bastard, how much do you owe?"

"Look..."

"No, you look." Patrick had hold of him by the lapels of his coat. "I know him. He was busted in London last year, thrown out of Italy before that, jailed in Berlin. He's a user and a dealer, the worst kind of pimp there is."

"He's okay…"

Patrick pushed Val back against the bar. "He's not fucking okay. You hear me. Keep away from him. Unless you want to end up the same way."

On the small stage, the pianist was sounding a few chords, trying out a few runs. "I've got to go," Val said, and Patrick released his grip.

All of Val's anger came out on stage, channelled first through a blistering "Cherokee", then a biting up-tempo blues that seemed as if it might never end.

Patrick left Paris the next day, but not before he'd set up a recording date for Val and the trio at the Pathé-Magellan studio. The producer's idea was to cut an album of standards, none of the takes too long and with Val sticking close to the melody, so that, with any luck, some might be issued as singles for the many juke boxes around. Val always claimed to be less than happy with the results, feeling restricted by the set-up and the selection of tunes. Easy listening, I suppose it might be called nowadays, dinner jazz, but it's always been one of my favourites, even now.

It was when we were leaving the studio after the last session that the pianist invited us to go along later with him and his girlfriend to hear Lester Young. Val was evasive. Maybe *oui*, maybe *non*. The one night off from Le Chat, he might just crash, catch up on some sleep.

"I thought he was one of your favourites," I said, as we were heading for the Metro. "How come you didn't want to go?"

Val gave a quick shake of the head. "I hear he's not playing too well."

Young, I found out later, had already been in Paris for several weeks, playing at the Blue Note on the rue d'Artois and living at the Hotel La Louisiane. A room on the second floor he rarely if ever left except to go to work.

Val had brought a few records with him from England, one of them an LP with a tattered cover and a scratch across one side: Lester Young, some fifteen years earlier, in his prime.

Val sat cross-legged on his bed, listening to the same tracks again and again. I poured what remained of a bottle of wine and took my glass across to a chair opposite the door; traffic noise rose and faded through the partly opened shutters, the occasional voice raised in anger or surprise; the sound of the saxophone lithe and muscular in the room.

When the stylus reached the run-off groove for the umpteenth time, Val reached over and set his glass on the floor. "Okay," he said. "Let's take a chance."

As we entered the club and walked past the long bar towards the stage, a tune I failed to recognise came to an end and Young, caught in the spotlight, stared out, startled, as the applause riffled out above the continuing conversation. Up close, he looked gaunt and ill, dark suit hanging ragged from his shrunken frame, pain all too visible behind his eyes.

I took hold of Val's hand and squeezed it hard.

The drummer kicked off the next number at a brisk clip, playing quick patterns on the hi-hat cymbals with his sticks before moving to the snare, a signal for Young, saxophone tilted at an angle away from his body, to begin. Within the first bars, he had dragged the tempo down, slurring his notes across the tune, the same stumbling phrases repeated and then left hanging as he stepped back and caught his breath, the spaces between his playing wider and wider until finally he turned away and stood, head bowed, leaving the guitarist to take over.

"I Can't Get Started" was played at a funeral pace, the sound coarse and almost ugly; "Tea for Two", one of the tunes

26

Val had been listening to back in the hotel, started promisingly before teetering alarmingly off course; only a measured "There Will Never Be Another You" rose from its foggy, thick-breathed beginning to become something that had moments of beauty between the self-doubt and misfingerings.

"If I ever get into that state, poor bastard," Val said, once we were back outside, "promise you'll take me out and shoot me."

Yet in the succeeding weeks he went back again, not once but several times, fascinated despite himself, watching one of his idols unravel before his eyes. Then there was the time he went along and Young was no longer there; he'd cancelled his engagement suddenly and returned to the States. Two weeks later he was dead.

The evening he heard the news Val played "There Will Never Be Another You", just the one chorus, unaccompanied, at the beginning of each set. The day later I walked into his room in the middle of the afternoon, and saw him sitting, half-naked on the bed, needle in hand, searching for a vein.

"Oh, Christ, Val," I said.

He looked at me with tears in his eyes then slapped the inside of his thigh again.

I slammed the door shut, grabbed my coat and purse and ran out on to the street. For hours I just walked, ending up who knows where. At a corner bar I drank two brandies in quick succession followed by a crème de menthe and was promptly sick. I wanted to go back to the hotel, pack my bag and leave. What the hell was I doing there? What game? What stupid dream? There was vomit on the hem of my dress and on my shoes.

When finally I got to the club it was late and Val was nowhere to be seen, just his saxophone, mouthpiece covered, on its stand. In answer to my unspoken question, the pianist just shrugged and, still playing, gestured with his head towards the street.

I heard Val's shouts, muffled, coming from the alley that ran from close alongside the club down towards the Quai Saint-Michel. Val lay curled in on himself, arms cradling his head, while two men took it in turns to kick him in the back, the chest, the legs, anywhere they could, a third looking on.

"Espèce d'ordure, je vais te crever la paillasse!"

I stood, frozen, unable to react, then ran forward, screaming, and, as I threw myself at one of the men, he swung his arm into my face and I went stumbling back against the wall, blood filling my mouth. The sound of police sirens was too indistinct, too far away.

When someone helped me to my feet and I walked, unsteadily, to where Val still lay, unmoving, I thought that they had killed him. I thought he was dead.

For three days I sat by his bed in the hospital and held his hand. At night, I slept in the corridor outside, legs drawn up, on a chair. One of several broken ribs had come close to puncturing a lung. A week later I held his hand again as we walked in the hospital garden, bare earth and the stems of roses that had been cut back against the frost.

"How are you feeling?" I asked him.

"Fine," he said, wincing as he smiled. "I feel fine."

After that there were always dull headaches that prevented him from sleeping and sudden surges of pain, sharp as a needle slipped beneath the skull. Despite the months and years of osteopathy, his back never sat right again, nagging at him each time he played.

Valentine Collins, jazz musician. Born, September 18th, 1937. Died, April 13th, 1976. Thirty years ago. No need any longer to take the ferry to Calais and then the long, slow journey by train, and not caring to fly, I treated myself to Eurostar, first class. A slightly better than aeroplane meal and free Champagne. The centre of Paris in less than three hours. Autumn. The bluest of blue skies but cold enough for scarf and gloves. I feel the cold.

The Metro from Gare du Nord to Saint-Michel is crowded with so many races, so many colours, Val's face would not have stood out at all. Not one of us, Patrick had said, and it was true, though not in the way he meant.

The rue de la Huchette is now a rat-run of kebab houses and crêperies and bars, so crowded, here and there I have to walk along the centre of the narrow street.

Le Chat Qui Pêche is now a restaurant and the sign has been taken down. For a while I think I might go inside and have a meal, reminisce a little with the waiter, if he has a little English to complement my meagre French. But it is enough to stand here at the pavement's edge with people spilling round me, wondering, some of them, perhaps, what this old woman is doing, just standing there, staring at nothing in particular, none of them hearing what I hear, the sound of Val's alto saxophone, a ballad, astringent, keening, "Every Time We Say Goodbye".

Billie's Blues

Angels, that was what he thought. The way she lay on her back, arms spread wide, as if making angels in the snow. The front of her coat tugged aside, feet bare, the centre of her dress stained dark, fingers curled. A few listless flakes settled momentarily on her face and hair. Porcelain skin. In those temperatures she could have been dead for hours or days. The pathologist would know.

Straightening, Resnick glanced at his watch. Three forty-five. Still a way off morning. Little over half an hour since the call had come through. Soon there would be arc lights, a generator, yellow tape, officers in coveralls searching the ground on hands and knees. As Anil Khan, crouching, shot off the first of many Polaroids, Resnick stepped aside. The broad expanse of The Forest rose behind them, broken by a ragged line of trees. The city's orange glow.

"The woman as called it in," Millington said, at his shoulder. "You'll likely want a word."

She was standing some thirty metres off, where the scrub of grass and the gravel of the parking area merged.

"A wonder she stayed around," Resnick said.

Millington nodded and lit a cigarette.

She was tall, taller than average, dark hair that at closer range was reddish-brown, brown leather boots which stopped below the knee, a sheepskin coat she pulled across herself protectively as Resnick came near. A full mouth from which most of the lipstick had been worn away, eyes like sea water, bluey-green. The fingers holding her coat close were raw with cold.

Still Resnick did not recognise her until she had fumbled in her pockets for a pack of cigarettes, a lighter, the flame small yet sudden, flaring before her eyes.

"Eileen? Terry's Eileen?"

She looked at him then. "Not any more."

It had been two years, almost to the day, since the last time he had seen her, trapped out in widow's weeds. Since then, the seepage that had followed Terry Cooke's funeral had submerged her from Resnick's sight. Cooke, a medium-range chancer who had punched his weight but rarely more — aggravated burglary, the occasional lorry hi-jack, once a pay-roll robbery of almost splendid audacity — and who had ended his own life with a bullet through the brain, administered while Eileen lay in bed alongside him.

"You found her." Resnick's head nodded back in the direction of the corpse.

As a question, it didn't require answer.

"How come?"

"She was there, wasn't she? Lyin' there. I almost fell over her."

"I mean, three in the morning, how come you were here? On The Forest?"

"How d'you think?"

Resnick looked at her, waiting.

She gouged the heel of her boot into the frozen ground. "Business. What else?"

"Christ, Eileen."

"I was here doin' business."

"I didn't know."

"Why should you?" For the space of seconds, she looked back at him accusingly.

Resnick had talked to her several times in the weeks before Terry Cooke had died, Eileen seeking a way out of the relationship but too scared to make the move. And Resnick listening sympathetically, hoping she would give him an angle, a way of breaking through Cooke's camouflage and alibis. 'Give him up, Eileen. Give us something we can use. Once he's inside, he'll not be able to reach you, do you any harm.' In the end, Resnick had thought, the only harm Cooke had done had been to himself. Now, looking at Eileen, he was less sure.

"I'm sorry," Resnick said.

"Why the hell should you be sorry?"

He shrugged, heavy shouldered. If he knew why he couldn't explain. Behind, the sound of transport pulling off the road, reinforcements arriving.

"When you first knew me, Terry too, I was stripping, right? This in't so very different." They both knew that wasn't so. "Besides, get to my age, those kind of jobs, prime ones, they can get few and far between."

She was what, Resnick thought, twenty-six, twenty-seven? Shy of thirty, to be sure. "You'd best tell me what happened," he said.

Eileen lit a fresh cigarette from the butt of the last. "This punter, he said he weren't going to use a condom, couldn't understand why an extra twenty didn't see it right. Chucked me out and drove off. I was walking up onto Forest Road, thought I might pick up a cab, go back into town. Which was when I saw her. Ducked through that first lot of bushes and there she was."

"You could have carried on walking," Resnick said. "Skirted round." At his back, he could hear Millington's voice, organising the troops.

33

"Not once I'd seen her."

"So you called it in."

"Had my mobile. Didn't take but a minute."

"You could have left her then."

"No, I couldn't." Her eyes fastened on his, challenging.

The pathologist was driving slowly across the pitted surface towards them, mindful of the paint work on his new Volvo.

"I'll get someone to take you to the station," Resnick said. "Get a statement. No sense you freezing out here any more than you have to."

Already he was turning away.

***

The dead woman was scarcely that: a girl, mid-teens. Below medium height and underweight; scars, some possibly self-inflicted, to her legs and arms; bruising across the buttocks and around the neck. The thin cotton of her dress was stuck to her chest with blood. Scratches to exposed parts of the body suggested that she could have been attacked elsewhere then dragged to the spot where she was found and dumped. No bag nor purse nor any other article she might have been carrying had been discovered so far. Preliminary examination suggested she had been dead not less than twenty-four hours, possibly more. Further tests on her body and clothing were being carried out.

Officers would be out on the streets around Hyson Green and The Forest with hastily reproduced photographs, talking to prostitutes plying their trade, stopping cars, knocking on doors. Others would be checking missing persons on the computer, contacting social services, those responsible for the care and custody of juveniles. If no one had come forward with an identification by the end of the day, public relations would release a picture to the press for the morning editions, push for the maximum publicity on local radio and TV.

In his office, Resnick eased a now lukewarm mug of coffee aside and reached again for the transcript of Lynn Kellogg's interview with Eileen. As a document in a murder investigation it was unlikely to set the pulses racing; Eileen's responses rarely rose above the monosyllabic, her description of her punter generalised, while Lynn's questioning, for once, was little more than routine.

In the CID room, Lynn Kellogg's head was just visible over the top of her VDU. Resnick waited until she had saved what was on the screen and dropped the transcript down on her desk.

"You didn't get on, you and Eileen."

"Were we supposed to?"

"You didn't like her."

"What was to like?"

A suggestion of a smile showed on Resnick's face. "She dialled 999. Hung around. Agreed to make a statement."

"Which was next to useless."

"Agreed."

Lynn touched her index finger to the keyboard and the image on the screen disappeared. "I'm sorry, sir, but what exactly's your point?"

"I'm just wondering if we've missed something, that's all."

"You want me to talk to her again?"

"Perhaps not."

Lynn's eyes narrowed perceptibly. "I see."

"I mean, if she sensed you didn't like her..."

"Whereas she might open up to you."

"It's possible."

With a slow shake of the head, Lynn flipped back through the pages of her notebook for the address and copied it onto a fresh sheet, which Resnick glanced at quickly before folding it down into the breast pocket of his suit.

"She's a tart, sir. A whore."

If, on his way to the door, Resnick heard her, he gave no sign.

***

It was a two-up, two-down off the Hucknall Road, opening into the living room directly off the street: one of those old staples of inner city living that are gradually being bulldozed from sight, some would say good riddance, to be replaced by mazes of neat little semis with miniature gardens and brightly painted doors.

Eileen answered the bell in jeans and a baggy sweat shirt, hair tied back, no trace of make-up on her face.

"Lost?" she asked caustically.

"I hope not."

She stood back and motioned him inside. The room was neat and comfortably furnished, a framed photograph of herself and Terry on the tiled mantelpiece, some sunny day in both their pasts. Set into the old fireplace, a gas fire was going full blast; the television playing soundlessly, racing from somewhere, Newmarket or Uttoxeter, hard going under leaden skies.

"Nice," Resnick said, looking round.

"But not what you'd've expected."

"How d'you mean?"

"Terry, leaving me half of everything. You'd have reckoned something posh, Burton Joyce at least."

"Maybe."

"Yes, well, half of everything proved to be half of nothing much. Terry, bless him, all over. And by the time that family of his had come scrounging round, to say nothing of all his mates, Frankie Farmer and the rest, oh, Terry owed me this, Terry promised me that, I was lucky to get away with what I did."

"You could always have said no, turned them down."

"You think so?" Eileen reached for her cigarettes, bent low and lit one from the fire. "Farmer and his like, 'no's' not a word they like to hear."

"They threatened you?"

Tilting back her head, she released a slow spiral of smoke towards the ceiling. "They didn't have to."

Nodding, Resnick began to unbutton his overcoat.

"You're stopping then?" Almost despite herself, a smile along the curve of her mouth.

"Long enough for a coffee, maybe."

"It's instant."

"Tea then." Resnick grinned. "If that's all right."

With a short sigh, Eileen held out her hand. "Here. Give me your coat."

She brought it through from the kitchen on a tray, the tea in mugs, sugar in a blue and white Tate & Lyle bag, three digestive biscuits, one of them chocolate-faced.

"You did want milk?"

"Milk's fine."

Eileen sat opposite him in the second of matching chairs, stirred two sugars into her tea, leaned back and lit another cigarette.

"The last thousand I had left..." she began.

"You don't have to tell me," Resnick said.

"What was I doing, out on The Forest, your question."

"You still don't have..."

"Maybe I do."

Resnick sat back and listened.

"The last thousand from what Terry left me — after I'd bought this place, I mean — this pal of mine — least, I'd reckoned her for a pal — she persuaded me to come in with her on this sauna she was opening, Mapperley Top. Money was for the deposit, first three months' rent, tarting the place up — you know, a lick of paint and a few posters — buying towels and the like." She rested her cigarette on the edge of the tray and swallowed a mouthful of tea. "Vice Squad raided us five times in the first fortnight. Whether it was one of the girls refusing a freebie or something more — back handers, you know the kind of thing — I never knew. Either way, a month after we opened we were closed and I was left sorting out the bills."

"I'm sorry."

"So you keep saying."

"Maybe it's true."

"And maybe it's you."

"How d'you mean?"

She gave a little snort of derision. "It's what you do. Your way of getting what you want. Kind word here, little smile there. All so bloody understanding. It's all bollocks, Charlie. You told me to call you that, remember? When you were buttering me up before, trying to use me to get Terry locked away."

Resnick held his tea in both hands, fingers laced around the mug, saying nothing.

"Well, I didn't. Wouldn't. Never would. But Terry didn't know that, did he? Saw you and me together and thought the worst. If you'd been screwing me, it wouldn't've been so bad, he could have coped with that, I reckon, come to terms. But no, he thought I was grassing him up. And that was what he couldn't live with. The thought that I was betraying him. So he topped himself."

Both of them knew it hadn't been that simple.

Tears had appeared at the corners of Eileen's eyes and with the back of her hand she brushed them away. "I reckon there was a lot of unsolved business written off that day, eh, Charlie? Anything that Terry might've had his hand in and a lot more besides. A lot of your blokes lining up to pat your back and buy you a drink and help you spit on Terry's grave."

Resnick waited until the worst of the anger had faded from her eyes. "I deserve that. Some of it."

"Yes, you bastard, you do."

"And I am…"

"Don't." She stretched a hand towards his face, fingers spread. "Just don't bother with sorry. Just tell me what you're doing here, sitting there in my front room, taking all that shit from me."

Resnick set his mug down on the tray. "The girl," he said, "the one whose body you found. I think there's something about her you're still keeping back."

"Christ!" Up on her feet, she paced the room. "I should've left her, shouldn't I? Poor stupid cow. Minded my own bloody business."

Resnick followed her with his eyes. "Stupid, Eileen. What way was she stupid?"

"She was a kid, a girl, I doubt she was old enough to have left school."

"You did know her then?"

"No."

"A kid, you said…"

"I saw her lyin' there, didn't I."

"And that was all?"

Eileen stood at the window, her breath warming circles on the glass. A heavy bass echoed faintly through the side wall, the same rhythm over and again. Traffic stuttered in and out of the city along the Hucknall Road.

"I saw her a few nights back," Eileen said. "Corner of Addison Street. Skirt up to her arse and four inch heels. She must've been freezing." Her back was still to Resnick, her voice clear in the small room. "This van had been up and down, two, maybe three times.

Blue van, small. Post office van, that sort of size. Just the one bloke inside. He'd given me the once over, going past real slow, the girl too. Finally he stops alongside her and leans out. I thought she was going to get in, but she didn't. To and fro about it for ages they was before he drives off and she goes back to her stand. Fifteen, twenty minutes later he's back, straight to her this time, no messing, and this time get in is what she does."

Eileen turned to face him, hands behind her pressed against the wall.

"A few nights back," Resnick said. "Is that three or four?"

"Three."

"Monday, then?"

"I suppose."

"The driver, you knew him?"

"No." The hesitation was slight, slight enough that Resnick, going over the conversation later, couldn't be certain it was his imagination.

"You're sure?"

"Course."

"And the van?"

She shook her head.

"The driver, though. You'd recognise him again?"

"I don't know. I might."

Resnick set the mug down on the tray, tea barely touched. "Thanks, Eileen. Thanks for your time."

She waited until he was at the door. "When the van came back the second time, I can't be sure, but I think there were two of them, two blokes, the second one leaning forward from the back. Like I say, I can't be sure."

The temperature seemed to have dropped another five degrees when Resnick stepped out from the comparative warmth of the house onto the street and clouds hung low overhead, laden with snow.

The pathologist was a short, solid man with stubby fingers that seemed unsuited to his daily tasks. Despite the cold, they stood at one corner of the parking area to the building's rear, Resnick and himself, allowing the pathologist to smoke.

"Weather, eh, Charlie."

Resnick grunted in reply.

"All right for you, up off the Woodborough Road; where I am, down by the Trent, bloody river freezes over, soon as the bugger thaws you're up to your ankles in flood water and baling out downstairs like the place has sprung a leak."

"The girl," Resnick nudged.

The pathologist grinned. "Hamlet, Charlie. Act one, scene two."

"Come again?"

"Had you down as a bit of a scholar. On the quiet at least. "Seems, madam? Nay, it is. I know not seems." That poor kid, stretched out in the snow, clothes stuck to her with blood, jumped to the same conclusions, you and me, I'll wager. Cut. Stabbed. Sliced." He sucked noisily on the end of his cigar. "Not a bit of it. Not her blood. Different type altogether. No, she was strangled, Charlie. Throttled. Bare hands. Likely passed out within minutes, that's one mercy. Bruising in plenty elsewhere, mind you, some consistent with being struck by a fist and some not. Something hard and narrow. Old-fashioned poker, something similar. And semen, Charlie, generous traces of, inside and out."

For a moment, without willing it, Resnick's eyes shut fast.

"Marks round her wrists," the pathologist continued, "as if at some point she'd been tied up. Tight enough to break the skin."

"Rope or metal?"

"Metal."

41

"Like handcuffs?"

"Very like."

Unbidden, instinctive, the scene was beginning to play out in Resnick's mind.

"One person's or more?" he asked. "The semen."

"I'll get back to you."

Resnick nodded. "Anything else?"

"Fragments of material beneath her finger nails. Possibly skin. It's being analysed now."

"How close can you pin down the time of death?"

"Likely not as close as you'd like."

"Try me."

"Twenty-four hours, give or take."

"So if she was killed elsewhere and then dumped…"

"Which everything else suggests."

"She'd likely been on The Forest since the early hours of Wednesday morning."

"Where she was found, not unfeasible." The pathologist stubbed out the last smoulderings of the cigar on the sole of his shoe. "Noon tomorrow, Charlie, I'll have more for you then."

Resnick cupped both hands together and lifted them to his face, breathing out warm air.

Back upstairs in the CID room, Lynn Kellogg was talking to a Mrs Marston from a village just north of Melton Mowbray, arranging for her and her husband to be picked up and driven into the city, there to assist in the identification of the body of a fifteen-year-old girl who corresponded to the description of their missing daughter.

***

Her name was Kate. She'd run away twice before without getting further than Leicester services on the M1. The usual things:

clothes, boys, forever missing the last bus home, the silver stud she'd had put through her nose, the ring she wanted through her navel. Fifteen years and three months. Pills. Sex. Her father ran a small-holding, found it hard; four mornings a week her mum worked in a newsagent in Melton, cycling the seven or so miles so she could open up first thing. Weekends they helped out at the local nature reserve, her mum made scones, coffee and walnut cake, the best.

"For Christ's sake," Resnick had said, "if it is her, don't tell them any more than they need to know."

Ashen faced, Tom Marston held his wife by the shoulders as she beat her fists against his chest, her screams of denial tearing the sterile air.

The morning papers were full of it. Schoolgirl sex. Prostitution. Murder. An ordinary family grieves. Photographs of Kate in her school uniform vied for space with close-ups of her parents, stolen with a telephoto lens. The police are seeking to trace the driver of a blue van, seen in the vicinity of Addison Street and Forest Road East.

The pathologist beat his deadline by close on an hour. DNA samples taken from the girl's body confirmed that the semen came from two different men, one of whom was the source of the blood that had soaked her dress. Scrapings of skin found beneath her fingernails were from the second man. Filaments of a muddy green synthetic material, also taken from under her nails, seemed to have come from cheap, generic carpeting.

Two men, one young girl. A room without windows, a locked door. Do they take it in turns, one watching through a peep hole while they other performs? A video camera? Polaroids? When she screams, as Resnick assumes she must, why are those screams not heard? And the handcuffs — is she cuffed to a bed or somehow to the floor?

Anil Khan took Eileen to Central Station and watched while

she went through book after book of mug shots, barely glancing at each page. Resnick was there on the spread of pavement when she left.

"Don't go out tonight, Eileen. Stay close to home."

He turned and watched as she continued on down Shakespeare Street towards the taxi rank on Mansfield Road.

**

Back in his own kitchen, the cats winding between his legs, anxious to be fed, Resnick poured himself a generous shot of scotch and drank it down, two swallows then a third. Blood on the walls. Was there blood on the walls? He forked tinned food into four bowls, poured water and milk. Officers had contacted Accident and Emergency at Queen's and the other hospitals, the only serious stab wounds seemingly the result of drunk and disorderly or domestics, but these were all being checked. He rinsed his hands beneath the tap before assembling a sandwich on slices of dark rye, grinding coffee. Skin beneath the girl's finger nails. Fighting back. Had she somehow got hold of a knife, seized it when, for whatever reason, the cuffs were undone? Or had there been a falling out between the two men? Jealousy? Fear?

The front room struck cold, the radiators likely in need of bleeding; switching on the light, Resnick pulled across the curtains, thankful for their weight. Why strangle her? Take her life. A fit of anger, irrational, unplanned? A response to being attacked? Somehow, had things gone too far, got out of hand? He crossed to the stereo where a CD still lay in place: Billie Holiday on Commodore. "I'll Be Seeing You". "Strange Fruit".

Less than forty minutes later, sandwich and coffee long finished, Billie's voice still ringing in his head, he prised the smallest cat from his lap, switched off the amplifier, lifted down

44

his top coat from the pegs in the hall, and went out to where the elderly Saab was parked alongside the house. Slowly, doubtless looking like a punter himself, he drove around the Forest, doubling back through a succession of interlocking streets until he was sure Eileen was not there. When, later, he passed her house, lights were burning upstairs and down.

His sleep was patchy and by five he was fully awake, listening to the breathing of the two cats entwined near the foot of his bed, the faint fall of snow against the pane.

They would have known, wouldn't they, that Eileen had seen the girl getting into their van.

***

Next morning, the snow on the streets was just a memory. Sunshine leaked, pale and weak, through clouds smeared purplish-grey. At the obligatory press conference, Resnick made a brief statement, responded to questions without ever really answering, showed a right and proper concern for the Marstons in their bereavement. "Good job," said the public relations officer approvingly as they left the platform. Resnick scowled.

The work was being done in the CID office, the incident room, men and women accessing computer files, cross-checking messages, transcripts of interviews. So easy to let things slip, fail to make the right connection, wrongly prioritise. In addition to the Sex Offenders' Register, they would check through the Vice Squad's list of men stopped and cautioned trawling the red light district in their cars. Married men. Business men. Men who were inadequate, law-abiding, lonely, unhinged. Men with a record of violence. Men who cuddled up to their wives each night in the matrimonial bed, never forgot an anniversary, a birthday, kissed the children and wished them happiness, sweet dreams.

Neither of the DNA samples taken from Kate Marston's body found a positive match. Follow-up calls relating to reported stab wounds yielded nothing.

Time passed.

Four days after the enquiry had begun, the burned-out skeleton of a blue Ford Escort van was found at the end of a narrow track near Moorgreen Reservoir, some dozen miles north-west of the city centre.

Late on the Sunday evening, as Resnick was letting himself back into the house after a couple of hours at the Polish Club, accordions and reminiscence, bison grass vodka, the phone rang in the hall. The sergeant out at Carlton wasted few words: name's Eileen, sir, hell of a state, asking for you.

Within minutes, driving with particular care, Resnick was heading south on Porchester Road, cutting through towards Carlton Hill.

***

She was pale, shaken, huddled inside a man's raincoat, the collar upturned. There were grazes to her face and hands and knees, a swelling high on her right temple; below her left cheekbone, a bruise slowly emerging like soft fruit. A borrowed sweater, several sizes too large, covered the silver snap-front uplift bra and matching g-string: she had got a job stripping after all. Her feet were bare. She had climbed out of the bathroom window of a house off Westdale Lane, jumped from the roof of the kitchen extension to the ground and fallen heavily, run through the side gate onto the road, throwing herself, more or less, in front of the first car which came along. The duty sergeant had calmed her down as best he could, taken a brief statement, provided tea and cigarettes.

Eileen saw Resnick with relief and tugged at his sleeve, her words tumbling over one another, breathlessly. "It was him. I

46

swear it. At the house."

"Which house? Eileen, slow down."

"Someone called, set up this private session, his brother's birthday. Half a dozen of them there, all blokes. Just as I was getting into it, he showed himself, back of the room. I don't know if he meant to, not then. Anyhow, I just panicked. Panicked and ran. Shut myself in the bathroom and locked the door behind me."

"And it was him, the driver from the van? You're certain?"

"Not the driver," Eileen said. "The other man."

"This address," Resnick said, turning towards the sergeant, "Off Westdale Lane, you've checked it out?"

"No, sir. Not as yet."

"Why in God's name not?"

"Way I saw it, sir, seeing as she'd asked for you, I thought to wait, just, you know, in case..."

"Get some people out there now. I doubt you'll find anyone still inside, but if you do, I want them brought in so fast their feet don't touch the ground. And get the place sealed. I'll want it gone over tomorrow with a fine-tooth comb. Knock up the neighbours, find out who lives there, anything else you can. Whatever you get, I want it passed through to me direct. Understood?"

"Yes, sir."

"Then snap to it."

Resnick turned towards Eileen. "Whoever made this booking, did he leave a name?"

"Phil."

"That was it?"

"Yes." Instead of looking at him now, she was staring at the floor. "There's something else," she said, her voice so quiet he could only just make out the words.

"Go on."

47

"Not here," she said, glancing round. "Not here."

Taking her arm, Resnick led Eileen outside to where the Saab was parked at the kerb. "I'll take you home. We can talk there."

"No." Fear in her eyes. "He knows, doesn't he? He knows where I live."

"Okay," Resnick said, holding open the car door. "Get in."

Less than ten minutes later they were standing in the broad hallway of Resnick's house, a small commotion of cats scurrying this way and that.

"Charlie..."

"Yes?" It still took him by surprise, the way she used his name.

"Before anything else, can I have a bath?"

"Of course. Follow the stairs round and it's on the left. I'll leave you a towel outside the door."

"Thanks."

"And that trick with the bathroom window," he called after her. "I wouldn't recommend it twice in the same evening."

Taking his time, he grilled bacon, sliced bread, broke eggs into a bowl; when he heard her moving around in the bathroom, the water running away, he forked butter into a small pan and turned the gas up high, adding shavings of Parmesan to the eggs before they set.

Eileen appeared in the kitchen doorway wearing an old dressing gown he scarcely ever bothered with, a towel twisted around her head.

"I thought you should eat," Resnick said.

"I doubt if I can."

But, sitting across from him at the kitchen table, she wolfed it down, folding a piece of the bread in half and wiping the last of the egg from her plate.

Uncertain, Pepper and Miles miaowed from a distance.

"Don't you feed them, Charlie?"

"Sometimes."

Eileen pushed away her plate. "You know what I need after that?"

"A cup of coffee?"

"A cigarette."

She stood in the rear doorway, looking out across the garden, a few stunted trees in silhouette and, beyond the wall, the land falling away into darkness.

Resnick rinsed dishes at the sink.

When she came back inside and closed the door behind her, her skin shone from the cold. "He's one of yours," she said.

Resnick felt the breath stop inside his body

"Vice, at least I suppose that's what he is. The sauna, that's where I saw him, just the once. With one of the girls. Knocked her around. Split her lip. It wasn't till tonight I was sure."

"You scarcely saw him in the van. You said so yourself."

"Charlie, I'm sure."

"So the description you gave before..."

"It was accurate, far as it went."

"And now?"

"He's got — I don't know what you'd call it — a lazy eye, the left. It sort of droops. Just a little. Maybe you'd never notice at first, but then, when you do ... The way he looks at you."

Resnick nodded. "The driver, did you see him there tonight as well?"

Eileen shook her head. "I don't know. No. I don't think so. I mean, he could've been, but no, I'm sorry, I couldn't say."

"It's okay." Now that the shock had faded, Resnick caught himself wondering why the allegation was less of a surprise than it was.

"You don't know him?" Eileen asked. "Know who he is?"

Resnick shook his head. "It won't take long to find out."

In the front room he sat in his usual chair and Eileen rested her back against one corner of the settee, legs pulled up beneath her, glass of scotch balancing on the arm.

"You'll go after him?"

"Oh, yes."

"On my word?"

"Yes."

She picked up her drink. "You'll need more than that, Charlie. In court. The word of a whore."

"Yes. Agreed."

The heating had clicked off and the room was slowly getting colder. He wondered why it didn't seem stranger, her sitting there. Refilling both their glasses, he switched on the stereo and, after a passage of piano, there was Billie's voice, half-broken...

I ain't good lookin' and my hair don't curl
I ain't good lookin' and my hair don't curl
But my mama she give me somethin',
gonna carry me through this world.

"Sounds like," Eileen said with a grin, "she knows what she's talking about."

Less than ten minutes later, she was stretching her arms and yawning. "I think I'll just curl up on here, if that's the same to you."

"No need. There's a spare room upstairs. Two."

"I'll be okay."

"Suit yourself. And if any of the cats jump up on you, push them off."

Eileen shook her head. "I might like the company."

It was a little after two when she climbed in with him, the dressing gown discarded somewhere between the door and the

50

bed. Startled awake, Resnick thrashed out with his arm and only succeeded in sending the youngest cat skittering across the floor.

"Charlie."

"Christ, Eileen!"

Her limbs were strong and smooth and cold.

"Eileen, you can't..."

"Shush."

She lay with one leg angled over his knee, an arm across his midriff holding him close, her head to his chest. Within minutes the rhythm of her breathing changed and she was asleep, her breath faint and regular on his skin.

How long, Resnick wondered, since he had lain with a woman like this, in this bed? When his fingers touched the place between her shoulder and her neck, she stirred slightly, murmuring a name that wasn't his.

It was a little while later before the cat felt bold enough to resume its place back on the bed.

"Is there anywhere you can go?" Resnick asked. "Till all this blows over."

"You mean, apart from here."

"Apart from here."

They were in the kitchen, drinking coffee, eating toast.

"Look, if it's last night..."

"No, it's not."

"I mean, it's not as if..."

"It's what you said yourself, at the moment everything's hanging on your word. It just needs someone to make the wrong connection between you and me..."

"Okay, you don't have to spell it out. I understand."

The radio was still playing, muffled, in the bathroom. Politics: the same evasions, the same lies. As yet the outside

51

temperature had scarcely risen above freezing, the sky several shades of grey.

"I've got a friend," Eileen said, "in Sheffield. I can go there." She glanced down at what she was now wearing, one of his shirts. A morning-after cliché. "Only I shall need some clothes."

"I'll drive you round to your place after breakfast, wait while you pack."

"Thanks."

Resnick drank the last of his coffee, pushed himself to his feet. "You'll let me have a number, in case I need to get in touch?"

"Yes. Yes, of course."

She took one more mouthful of toast and left the rest.

***

They were gathered together in Resnick's office, the clamour of the everyday going on behind its closed door: Graham Millington, Anil Khan and Sharon Garnett. Sharon had been a member of the Vice Squad before being reassigned to Resnick's team and had maintained her contacts.

"Burford," Sharon said once Resnick had relayed the description. "Jack Burford, it's got to be."

Millington whistled, a malicious glint in his eye. "Jack Burford — honest as the day is long."

It wasn't so far from the shortest day of the year.

"How well do you know him?" Resnick asked.

"Well enough," Sharon said. "We'd have a drink together once in a while." She laughed. "Never too comfortable in my company, Jack. A woman who speaks her mind and black to boot, more than he could comfortably handle. No, a bunch of the lads, prize fights, lock-ins and lap dancers, that was more Jack's mark. Gambling, too. In and out of Ladbroke's most afternoons."

52

"These lads, anyone closer to him than the rest?"

She gave it a few moments' thought. "Jimmy Lyons, if anyone."

"Left the force, didn't he?" Millington said. "About a year back. Early retirement or some such."

"There was an enquiry," Sharon said. "Allegations of taking money to turn a blind eye. Massage parlours, the usual thing. Didn't get anywhere."

"And they worked together," Resnick asked, "Burford and Lyons."

Sharon nodded. "Quite a bit."

"Lyons," Resnick said. "Anyone know where he is now?"

Nobody did.

"Okay. Sharon, chase up one or two of your contacts at Vice, those you think you can trust. See what the word is on Burford. Anil, see if you can track down Lyons. He might still be in the city somewhere, in which case he and Burford could still be in touch."

Millington was already at the door. "I'd best get myself out to Carlton, see how they're getting on. You'll want them dragging their feet on this."

By four it was pretty much coming into place. The carpet fibres found beneath Kate Marston's finger nails matched the floor covering throughout the upstairs of the house off Westdale Lane. And traces of blood, both on the carpet and in the bathroom, were identical with that on the girl's clothing.

The house had been let a little over two years back to a Mr and Mrs Mason, Philip and Dawn. None of the neighbours could recall seeing Dawn Mason for a good six months and assumed the couple had split up; since then Philip Mason had been sharing the place with his brother, John. John Mason was known to the police: a suspended sentence for grievous bodily harm eight years before and, more recently, a charge of rape which had been dropped by the CPS at the last moment because some of the evidence was considered unsafe. Unusually, the rape charge had been brought by a prostitute, who claimed Mason had threatened her with a knife and sodomised her against her will. What made it especially interesting — the arresting officers had been Burford and Lyons.

Lyons was still in the city, Khan confirmed, working with a security firm which provided bouncers for night clubs and pubs; rumour was that he and Burford were still close. And Lyons had not been seen at work since the night Kate Marston had been killed.

Resnick crossed to the deli on Canning Circus, picked up a large filter coffee and continued into the cemetery on the far side. Burford and Lyons or Burford and Mason, cruising The Forest in the van, looking for a likely girl. Finally, they get her back to the house and somewhere in the midst of it all things start to go awry.

He sat on a bench and levered the lid from his cup; the coffee was strong and still warm. It had to be Burford and Lyons who had sex with the girl; Mason's DNA was likely still on file and no match had registered. So what happened? Back on his feet again, Resnick started to walk down hill. Burford and Lyons are well into it when Mason takes it into his head to join in. It's Mason who introduces the knife. But whose blood? Jimmy Lyons' blood. He's telling Mason to keep out of it and Mason won't listen; they argue, fight, and Lyons gets stabbed, stumbles over the girl. Grabs her as he falls.

Then if she doesn't do the stabbing, why does she have to die?

She's hysterical and someone — Burford? — starts slapping her, shaking her, using too much force. Or simply this: she's seen too much.

Resnick sits again, seeing it in his mind. Is it now that she struggles and in desperation fights back? Whose skin then was with those carpet fibres, caught beneath her nails? He sat a little longer, finishing his coffee, thinking; then walked, more briskly, back towards the station. There were calls to make, arrangements to be put in place.

***

Burford spotted Sharon Garnett the second she walked into the bar, dark hair piled high, the same lift of the head, self-assured. It was when he saw Resnick behind her that he understood.

"Hello, Jack," Sharon said as she crossed behind him. "Long time."

Some part of Burford told him to cut and run, but no, there would be officers stationed outside he was certain, front and back, nothing to do now but play it through.

"Evening, Charlie. Long way off your turf. Come to see how the other half live?"

"Something like that."

"Get you a drink?"

"No, thanks."

"Sharon?"

Sharon shook her head.

"Suit yourself." Burford lifted the shot glass from the counter and downed what remained of his scotch in one.

Without any attempt to disguise what he was doing, Resnick picked up the glass with a clean handkerchief and deposited it in a plastic evidence bag, zipping the top across.

"Let's do this decent, Charlie," Burford said, taking a step away. "No cuffs, nothing like that. I'll just walk with you out to the car."

"Suit yourself," Resnick said.

"Decent," said Sharon. "That word in your vocabulary, Jack?"

Millington was outside in the car park, Anil Khan.

"You know I'm not saying a word without a solicitor," Burford said. "You know that."

"Shut up," Resnick said, "and get in the car."

When Lynn Kellogg hammered on the door of Jimmy Lyon's flat near the edge of the Lace Market, Lyons elbowed her aside and took off down the stairs smack into the arms of Kevin Naylor. Blood had already started to seep through the bandages across his chest.

John Mason had skipped town and his brother, Philip, claimed no knowledge of where he might be. "How about Mrs Mason?" Millington asked. "Been a while, I understand, since anyone's clapped eyes on her." Philip Mason turned decidedly pale.

Under questioning, both Burford and Lyons agreed to picking up Kate Marston and taking her back to the house for sex. They claimed they had left her alone in the upstairs room, which was where Mason, drunk, had threatened her with a knife and then attacked her. By the time they'd realised what was going on and ran back upstairs, he had his hands round her throat and she was dead. It was when Lyons tried to pull him off that Mason had stabbed him with the knife.

Marston claimed he then used his own car to take Lyons back to his flat and tended his wound. Mason, he assumed, carried the dead girl out to the van and left her on The Forest, disposing of the van afterwards.

Without Mason's side of things, it would be a difficult story to break down and Mason wasn't going to be easy to find.

***

About a week later, media interest in the case beginning to fade, Resnick left the Polish Club early, a light rain falling as he walked back across town. Indoors, he made himself a sandwich and poured the last of the scotch into a glass. Billie's voice was jaunty and in your face, even in defeat. Since the time she had sat across from him in his chair, slipped into his bed, he had never quite managed to shake Eileen from his mind. When he crossed the room and dialled again the number she had given him, the operator's message was the same: number unobtainable. The music at an end, the sound of his own breathing seemed to fill the room.

The Sun, the Moon
and the Stars

Eileen had done everything she could to change his mind. Michael, she'd said, anywhere else, okay? Anywhere but there. Michael Sandler not his real name, not even close. But in the end she'd caved in, just as he'd known she would. Thirty-three by not so many months and going nowhere; thirty-three, though she was still only owning up to twenty-nine.

When he'd met her she'd been a receptionist in a car showroom south of Sheffield, something she'd blagged her way into and held down for the best part of a year; fine until the head of sales had somehow got a whiff of her past employment, some potential customer who'd seen her stripping somewhere most likely, and tried wedging his podgy fingers up inside her skirt one evening late. Eileen had kneed him in the balls, then hit him with a solid glass ashtray high across the face, close to taking out an eye. She hadn't bothered waiting for her cards.

She'd been managing a sauna, close to the city centre, when Michael had found her. In at seven, check the towels, make sure the plastic had been wiped down, bottles of massage oil topped up, the come washed from the walls; once the girls arrived, first shift, ready to catch the early punters on their way to work,

59

she'd examine their hands, ensure they'd trimmed their nails; uniforms they took home and washed, brought back next day clean as new or she'd want the reason why.

"Come on," Michael had said, "fifty minutes down the motorway. It's not as if I'm asking you to fucking emigrate." Emigration might have been easier. She had memories of Nottingham and none of them good. But then, looking round at the tatty travel posters and old centrefolds from *Playboy* on the walls, he'd added: "What? Worried a move might be bad for your career?"

It hadn't taken her long to pack her bags, turn over the keys.

Fifty minutes on the motorway.

A house like a barn, a palace, real paintings on the walls.

When he came home earlier than usual one afternoon and found her sitting in the kitchen, polishing the silver while she watched Richard and Judy on the small TV, he snatched the cloth from her hands. "There's people paid for that, not you."

"It's something to do."

His nostrils flared. "You want something to do, go down the gym. Go shopping. Read a fucking book."

"Why?" she asked him later that night, turning towards him in their bed.

"Why what?"

"Why am I here?"

He didn't look at her. "Because I'm tired of living on my own."

He was sitting propped up against pillows, bare-chested, thumbing through the pages of a climbing magazine. Eileen couldn't imagine why: anything more than two flights of stairs and he took the lift.

The light from the lamp on his bedside table shone a filter of washed-out blue across the patterned quilt and the curtains stirred in the breeze from the opened window. One thing he insisted on, one of many, sleeping with at least one of the windows open.

"That's not enough," Eileen said.

"What?"

"Enough of a reason for me being here. You being tired of living alone."

After a long moment, he put down his magazine. "It's not the reason, you know that."

"Do I?" She leaned back as he turned towards her, his fingers touching her arm.

"I'm sorry about earlier," he said. "Snapping at you like that. It was stupid. Unnecessary."

"It doesn't matter."

"Yes, it does."

His face was close to hers, too close for her to focus; there was a faint smell of brandy on his breath.

After they'd made love he lay on his side, watching her, watching her breathe.

"Don't," she said.

"Don't what?"

"Don't stare. I hate it when you stare." It reminded her of Terry, her ex, the way his eyes had followed her whenever he thought she wasn't looking; right up until the night he'd slipped the gun out from beneath the pillow and, just when she'd been certain he was going to take her life, had shot himself in the head.

"What else am I supposed to do?" Michael said.

"Go to sleep? Take a shower?" Her face relaxed into a smile. "Read a fucking book?"

Michael grinned and reached across and kissed her. "You want to know how much I love you?"

"Yeah, yeah." Mocking.

After a little searching, he found a ballpoint in the bedside table drawer. Reaching for the magazine, he flicked through it till he came to a picture of the Matterhorn, outlined against the sky.

"Here," he said, and quickly drew a hasty, childlike approximation of the sun, moon and stars around the summit. "That's how much."

Smiling, Eileen closed her eyes.

Resnick had spent the nub end of the evening in a pub off the A632 between Bolsover and Arkwright Town. Peter Waites and himself. From the outside it looked as if the place had been closed down months before and the interior was not a lot different. Resnick paced himself, supping halves, aware of having to drive back down, while Waites worked his way assiduously from pint to pint, much as he had when he'd been in his pomp and working at the coal face, twenty years before.

Whenever it came to Waites' round, Resnick was careful to keep his wallet and his tongue well zipped, the man's pride buckled enough. He had lost his job in the wake of the miners' strike and not worked steady since.

"Not yet forty when they tossed me on the fuckin' scrap heap, Charlie. Me and a lot of others like me. Nigh on a thousand when that pit were closed and them pantywaist civil bloody servants chucking their hands up in the air on account they've found sixty new jobs. Bloody disgrace."

He snapped the filter from the end of his cigarette before lighting up.

"Lungs buggered enough already, Charlie. This'll not make ha'porth of difference, no matter what anyone says. Besides, long as I live long enough to see the last of that bloody woman and dance on her bloody grave, I don't give a sod."

That bloody woman: Margaret Hilda Thatcher.

In that company especially, no need to speak her name.

When they stepped outside the air bit cold. Over the care-fully sculpted slag heap, now slick with grass, the moon hung bright and full. Of the twenty terraced houses in Peter Waites' street, fourteen were now boarded up.

"You'll not come in, Charlie?"

"Some other time."

"Aye." The two men shook hands.

"Look after yourself, Peter."

"You, too."

Resnick had first met the ex-miner when his son had joined the Notts force as a young PC and been stationed for a while at Canning Circus, under Resnick's wing. Now the boy was in Australia, married with kids, something in IT, and Resnick and Waites still kept in touch, the occasional pint, an odd Saturday at Bramhall Lane or down in Nottingham at the County ground, a friendship based on mutual respect and a sense of regret for days gone past.

Eileen would never be sure what woke her. The flap of the curtain as the window opened wider; the soft tread on the carpeted floor. Either way, when she opened her eyes there they were, two shrouded shapes beyond the foot of the bed. Beside her, Michael was already awake, pushing up on one elbow, hand reaching out towards the light.

"Leave it," said a voice.

Already the shapes beginning to flesh out, take on detail.

"We don't need the fucking light," the shorter one said. A voice Eileen didn't recognise: one she would never forget.

Michael switched on the light and they shot him, the tall one first and then the other, the impact hurling Michael back against the headboard, skewing him round until his face finished somehow pressed up against the wall.

Moving closer, the shorter of the two wrenched the wire from the socket and the room went dark. Too late to prevent Eileen from seeing what she had seen: the taller man bareheaded, more than bare, shaven, bald, a child's mask, Mickey Mouse, covering the centre of his face; his companion had a woollen hat pulled low, a red scarf wrapped high around his neck and jaw.

Some of Michael's blood ran, slow and warm, between Eileen's arm and her breast. The rest was pooling between his legs, spreading dark across the sheets. The sound she hadn't recognised was her own choked sobbing, caught like a hairball in her throat. She knew they would kill her or rape her or both.

"You want it?" the shorter one said, gesturing towards the bed.

The tall one made a sound like someone about to throw up and the shorter one laughed.

Eileen closed her eyes and when she opened them again they had gone.

Welcoming the rare chance of an early night, Lynn had been in bed for a good hour by the time Resnick returned home. Through several layers of sleep she registered the Saab slowing into the drive outside, the front door closing firmly in its frame, feet slow but heavy on the stairs; sounds from the bathroom and then his weight on the mattress as he lowered himself down. More than two years now and she still sometimes felt it strange, this man beside her in her bed. His bed, to be more precise.

"God, Charlie," she said, shifting her legs. "Your feet are like blocks of ice. And you stink of beer."

His mumbled apology seemed to merge with his first snore.

His feet might be cold, but the rest of him seemed to radiate warmth. Lynn moved close against him and within not so many minutes she was asleep again herself.

Short of four, the phone woke them both.

"Yours or mine?" Resnick said, pushing back the covers.

"Mine."

She was already on her feet, starting to pull on clothes.

"Shooting," she said, when she'd put the phone back down. "Tattershall Drive."

"You want me to come?"

Lynn shook her head. "No need. Go back to sleep."

When they'd started living together, Lynn had transferred from Resnick's squad into Major Crime; less messy that way. Her coat, a hooded black anorak, windproof and waterproof, was on a hook in the hall. Despite the hour, it was surprisingly light outside, not so far off a full moon.

The body had not yet been moved. Scene of Crime were taking photographs, measuring, assiduously taking samples from the floor. The pathologist was still on his way. It didn't need an expert, Lynn thought, to see how he'd died.

Anil Khan stood beside her in the doorway. He had been the first officer from the Major Crime Unit to arrive.

"Two of them, so she says." His voice was light, barely accented.

"She?"

"Wife, mistress, whatever. She's downstairs."

Lynn nodded. When she had been promoted, three months before, detective sergeant to detective inspector, Khan had slipped easily into her shoes.

"Any idea how they got in?"

"Bedroom window, by the look of things. Out through the front door."

Lynn glanced across the room. "Flew in then, like Peter Pan?"

Khan smiled. "Ladder marks on the sill."

Eileen was sitting in a leather armchair, quilt round her shoulders, no trace of colour in her face. Someone had made her a cup of tea and it sat on a lacquered table, untouched. The room itself was large and unlived in, heavy dark furniture, dark paintings in ornamental frames; wherever they'd spent their time, Lynn thought, it wasn't here.

She lifted a high-backed wooden chair and carried it across the room. Through the partly open door she saw Khan escorting the pathologist towards the stairs. She set the chair down at an angle, close to Eileen, and introduced herself, name and rank. Eileen continued to stare into space, barely registering that she was there.

"Can you tell me what happened?" Lynn said.

No reply.

"I need you to tell me what happened," Lynn said. For a moment, she touched Eileen's hand.

"I already did. I told the Paki."

"Tell me. In your own time."

Eileen looked at her then. "They killed him. What more d'you want to know?"

"Everything," Lynn said. "Everything."

His name was Michael Sandler: Mikhail Sharminov. He had come to England from Russia fifteen years before. Born in Tibilisi, Georgia to Russo-Armenian parents, as a young man he had quickly decided a life devoted to the production of citrus fruits and tung oil was not for him. He went, as a student, to Moscow, and by the time he was thirty he had a thriving business importing bootlegged rock music through East Germany into Russia, everything from the Beatles to Janis Joplin. Soon, there were video tapes, bootlegged also: *Apocalypse Now*, *The Godfather*, *ET*. By the standards of the Russian black economy, Mikhail was on his way to being rich.

But then, by 1989 the Berlin Wall was crumbling and, in its wake, the Union of Soviet Socialist Republics was falling apart.

Georgia, where his ageing parents still lived, was on the verge of civil war. Free trade loomed.

Go or stay?

Mikhail became Michael.

In Britain he used his capital to build up a chain of provincial video stores, most of whose profits came from pirated DVDs; some of his previous contacts in East Berlin were now in Taiwan, in Tirana, in Hong Kong. Truly, a global economy.

Michael Sandler, fifty-eight years old. The owner outright of property to the value of two million five, together with the leases of more than a dozen stores; three bank accounts, one offshore; a collection of paintings, including a small Kandinsky worth an estimated eight hundred and fifty thousand pounds; three cars, a Lexus and two BMWs; four .38 bullets, fired from close range, two high in the chest, one to the temple, one that had torn through his throat.

Most of this information Lynn Kellogg amassed over the following days and weeks, piecing together local evidence with what could be gleaned from national records and H.M. Customs and Excise. And long before that, before the end of that first attenuated conversation, she realised she had seen Eileen before.

"Charlie," she said, phoning him at home. "I think you'd better get over here after all."

The first time Resnick had set eyes on Eileen, she'd been sitting in a basement wine bar, smoking a cigarette and drinking Bacardi and Coke, her hair redder then and falling loose around her shoulders. The harshness of her make-up, in that attenuated light, had been softened; her silver-grey top, like pale filigree, shimmered a little with each breath she took. She knew he was staring at her and thought little of it: it was what people did. Men, mostly. It was what, until she taken up with Terry Cooke, had paid her way in the world.

The sandwich Resnick had ordered arrived and when he bit into it mayonnaise smeared across the palm of his hand; through the bar stereo Parker was stripping the sentiment from "Don't Blame Me" — New York City, 1947, the closing bars of Miles' muted trumpet aside, it's Bird's alto all the way, acrid and languorous, and when it's over there's nothing left to do or say.

"You bastard!" Eileen had yelled later. "You fucking bastard! Making out you're so fucking sympathetic and understanding and all the while you're screwing me just as much as those bastards who think for fifty quid they can bend me over some car park wall and fuck me up the arse."

A nice turn of phrase, Eileen, and Resnick, while he might have resisted the graphic nature of her metaphor, would have had to admit she was right. He had wanted to apply pressure to Terry Cooke and his burgeoning empire of low-grade robbers and villains, and in Eileen, in what he had misread as her weakness, he thought he had seen the means.

"Leave him," he'd said. "Give us something we can make stick. Circumstances like this, you've got to look out for yourself. No one would blame you for that."

In the end it had been Terry who had weakened and whether it had been his fear of getting caught and being locked away that had made him pull the trigger, or his fear of losing Eileen, Resnick would never know. After the funeral, amidst the fallout and recriminations, she had slipped from sight and it was some little time before he saw her again, close to desperate and frightened, so frightened that he had offered her safe haven in that same big sprawling house where he now lived with Lynn, and there, in the long sparse hours between sleeping and waking, she had slid into his bed and fallen fast asleep, one of her legs across his and her head so light against his chest it could almost have been a dream.

Though his history of relationships was neither extensive nor particularly successful, and though he prized honesty above most other things, he knew enough never to have mentioned this incident to Lynn, innocent as he would vainly have tried to make it seem.

He stood now in the doorway, a bulky man with a shapeless suit and sagging eyes, and waited until, aware of his presence, she turned her head.

"Hello, Eileen."

The sight of him brought tears to her eyes. "Christ, Charlie. First Terry and now this. Getting to be too much of a fucking habit, if you ask me."

She held out a hand and he took it, and then she pressed her head against the rough weave of his coat, the too soft flesh beneath, and cried. After several moments, Resnick rested his other hand against her shoulder, close to the nape of her neck, and that's how they were some minutes later when Lynn looked into the room through the open door, then looked away.

"What did she have to say for herself?" Lynn asked. They were high on The Ropewalk, the light breaking through the sky, bits and pieces of the city waking south and west below them.

"No more, I dare say, than she told you," Resnick said.

"Don't tell me all that compassion went for nothing."

Resnick bridled. "She'd just seen her bloke shot dead alongside her, what was I supposed to do?"

Lynn gave a small shake of the head. "It's okay, Charlie. Just teasing."

"I'm glad to hear it."

"Though I do wonder if you had to look as if you were enjoying it quite as much."

At the end of the street they stopped. Canning Circus police station, where Resnick was based, was only a few minutes away.

"What do you think?" Lynn asked. "A paid hit?"

"I doubt it was a couple of local tearaways out to make a name for themselves. Whoever this was, they'll be well up the motorway by now. Up or down."

"Someone he'd crossed."

"Likely."

"Business, then."

"Whatever that is."

Lynn breathed in deeply, drawing the air down into her lungs. "I'd best get started."

"Okay."

"See you tonight."

"Yes."

She stood for a moment, watching him walk away. Her imagination, or was he slower than he used to be? Turning, she retraced her steps to where she'd parked her car.

Much of the next few days Lynn spent accessing and exchanging information on the computer and speaking on the telephone, building up, as systematically as she could, a picture of Mikhail Sharminov's activities, while forensic staff analysed the evidence provided by Scene of Crime.

At the start of the following week, Lynn, armed with a bulging brief case and a new Next suit, went to a meeting at the headquarters of the Specialist Crime Directorate in London; also present were officers from the National Criminal Intelligence Service and the National Crime Squad, as well as personnel from H.M. Customs and Excise, and observers from the Interpol team that was carrying out a long-term investigation into the Russian mafia.

By the time the meeting came to a halt, some six hours and several coffee breaks later, Lynn's head was throbbing with unfamiliar names and all-too-familiar motivations. Sharminov, it seemed, had been seen as an outsider within the Soviet diaspora; as far as possible he had held himself apart, relying instead on his contacts in the Far East. But with the increased capability for downloading not only CDs but now DVDs via the Internet, the logistics of his chosen field were changing, markets were shifting and becoming more specialised. There was a burgeoning trade in hard-core pornography which certain of Sharminov's former compatriots were keen to further through the networks he'd established. For a price. It wasn't clear whether he had resisted on moral grounds or because the price wasn't right.

Eileen was questioned at length about Sharminov's business partners and shown numerous photographs, the faces in which, for the most part, she failed to recognise. One man, middle-aged, with dark close-cropped hair and eyes too close together, had been to the house on several occasions, hurried conversations behind closed doors; another, silver-haired and leonine, she remembered seeing once, albeit briefly, in the rear seat of a limousine. There were others, a few, of whom she was less certain.

"Did he seem worried lately?" they asked her. "Concerned about business?"

"No," she said. "Not especially."

Perhaps he should have been. The silver-haired man was Alexei Popov, whose organisation encompassed drugs and pornography and human trafficking in a network that stretched from the Bosporus and the Adriatic to the English Channel, and had particularly strong links with the Turkish and Italian mafia. Tony Christanidi was his go-between and sometime enforcer, the kind of middle-management executive who never left home without first checking that his two-shot .22 Derringer was snug alongside his mobile phone.

The line back through Christanidi to Popov was suspected of being behind three recent fatal shootings, one in Manchester, one in Marseilles, the other in Tirana.

"Would they carry out these shootings themselves?" Lynn had asked.

"Not usually. Sometimes they'll make a deal with the Turks or the Sicilians. You do one for me, I'll do one for you. Other times, they'll simply contract it out. Usually overseas. Someone flies in, picks up the weapons locally, junks them straight after, twelve hours later they're back on the plane."

"So they wouldn't necessarily be English?"

"Not at all."

"The two men who shot Sharminov, the only witness we have swears they were English."

"This is the girlfriend?"

"Eileen. Yes."

"I don't understand."

"What?"

"Why they didn't kill her too."

"You don't think she could have been involved?"

"In setting him up? I suppose it's possible."

They questioned Eileen again, pushed her hard until her confidence was in shreds and her voice was gone.

"I don't think she knows anything," the National Crime Squad officer said after almost four hours of interrogation. "She was just lucky, that's all."

She wasn't the only one. Good luck and bad. In the early hours of the morning, almost two weeks and two days after Mikhail Sharminov was murdered, there was a shooting in the city. At around two in the morning, there was an altercation at the roundabout linking Canal Street with London Road, a Range Rover cutting across a BMW and causing the driver to brake hard. After a lot of gesturing and angry shouting, the

Range Rover drove off at speed, the other vehicle following. At the lights midway along Queen's Drive, where it runs beside the Trent, the BMW came alongside and the man in the passenger seat leaned out and shot the driver of the Range Rover five times.

The driver was currently in critical condition in hospital, hanging on.

Forensics suggested that the shots had been fired from one of the same weapons that had been used to kill Mikhail Sharminov, a snub-nosed .38 Smith and Wesson.

"It could mean whoever shot Sharminov was recruited locally after all," Lynn said. "Didn't see any need to leave town."

They were in the kitchen of the house in Mapperley, Saturday afternoon: Lynn ironing, a glass of white wine close at hand; Resnick putting together a salad with half an ear cocked towards the radio, the soccer commentary on Five Live.

"Well, he has now," Resnick said, wondering why the bottle of walnut oil was always right at the back of the cupboard when you needed it. Neither the driver nor passenger of the BMW had so far been traced.

"You think it's possible?" Lynn said.

Resnick shook a few drops of the oil over rocket and romaine and reached for the pepper. "I think you're on safer ground following the gun." He broke off a piece of lettuce to taste, scowled, and began ferreting for the Tabasco.

"Don't make it too hot, Charlie. You always do."

"Assume they've flown in. Birmingham, Leeds-Bradford, East Midlands. There's a meeting with whoever's supplying the weapons, prearranged. After the job, either they're dumped or, more likely, handed back."

"Recycled."

"I could still tell you which pub to go to if you wanted a converted replica. A hundred in tens handed over in the Gents. But this is a different league."

"Bernard Vitori," Lynn said. "He's the best bet. Eddie Chambers, possibly. One or two others. We'll start with Vitori first thing."

"Sunday morning?" Resnick said. "He won't like that."

"Disturbing his day of rest?"

"Takes his mother to church. Strelley Road Baptists. Regular as clockwork." Resnick ran a finger round the inside of the salad bowl. "Here. Taste this. Tell me what you think."

They followed Vitori and his mum to church, thirty officers, some armed, keeping the building tightly surrounded, mingling inside. The preacher was delighted by the increase in his congregation. Sixty or so minutes of energetic testifying later, Vitori reluctantly unlocked the boot of his car. Snug inside were a 9mm Glock 17 and a Chinese made A15 semi-automatic rifle. Vitori had been taking them to a potential customer after the service. Faced with the possibility of eight to ten inside, he cut a deal. Contact with the Russians had been by mobile phone, using numbers which were now untraceable, names which were clearly fake. Vitori had met two men in the Little Chef on the A60, north of Arnold. Leased them two clean revolvers for twenty-four hours, seven hundred the pair. Three days later, he'd sold one of the guns to a known drug dealer for five hundred more.

No matter how many times officers from Interpol and NICS showed him photographs of potential hit men, Vitori claimed to recognise none. He was not only happy to name the dealer, furnishing an address into the bargain, he gave them a likely identity for the driver of the car. Remanded in custody, special pleading would get him a five year sentence at most, of which he'd serve less than three.

'Bloody Russians, Charlie," Peter Waites said, sitting opposite Resnick in their usual pub. "When I was a kid we were always waiting for them to blow us up. Now they're over here like fucking royalty."

Sensing a rant coming, Resnick nodded noncommittally and supped his beer.

"That bloke owns Chelsea football club. Abramovich? He's not the only one, you know. This Boris, for instance — what's his name? — Berezovsky. One of the richest people in the fucking country. More money than the fucking Queen."

Resnick sensed it was not the time to remind Waites that as a dedicated republican, he thought Buckingham Palace should be turned into council housing and Her Majesty forced to live out her remaining years on her old age pension.

"You know how many Russians there are in this country, Charlie? According to the last census?"

Resnick shook his head. Waites had been spending too much time in Bolsover library, trawling the internet for free. "I give up, Peter," he said. "Tell me."

"Forty thousand, near as damn it. And they're not humping bricks for a few quid an hour on building sites or picking cockles in Morecambe fucking Bay. Living in bloody luxury, that's what they're doing." Leaning forward, Waites jabbed a finger urgently towards Resnick's face. "Every third property in London sold to a foreign citizen last year went to a bloody Russian. Every fifteenth property sold for over half a million the same." He shook his head. "This country, Charlie. Last ten, twenty years, it's turned upside fucking down." He wiped his mouth with the back of his hand.

"Another?" Resnick said, pointing to Waites' empty glass.

"Go on. Why not?"

For a good ten minutes neither man spoke. Noise and smoke spiralled around them. Laughter but not too much of that. The empty trill of slot machines from the far side of the bar.

"This soccer thing, Charlie," Waites said eventually. "Yanks buying into Manchester United and now there's this President of Thailand or whatever, wants forty per cent of Liverpool so's he can flog Steven Gerrard shirts and Michael Owen boots all over South-East Asia. It's not football any more, Charlie, it's all fucking business. Global fuckin' economy." He drank deep and drained his glass. "It's the global fucking economy as has thrown me and hundreds like me onto the fucking scrap heap, that's what it's done." Waites sighed and shook his head. "Sorry, Charlie. You ought never to have let me get started."

"Stopping you'd take me and seven others."

"Happen so."

At the door Waites stopped to light a cigarette. "You know what really grates with me, Charlie? It used to be a working class game, football. Now they've took that from us as well."

"Some places," Resnick said, "it still is."

"Come on, Charlie. What's happening, you don't think it's right no more'n me."

"Maybe not. Though I wouldn't mind some oil billionaire from Belarus taking a fancy to Notts County for a spell. Buy 'em a half-way decent striker, someone with a bit of nous for midfield."

Waites laughed. "Now who's whistling in the dark?"

For several months Customs and Excise and others did their best to unravel Sharminov's financial affairs; his stock was seized, his shops closed down. A further six months down the line, Alexei Popov would buy them through a twice-removed subsidiary and begin trading in DVDs for what was euphemistically called the adult market. He also bought a flat in

Knightsbridge for a cool five million, close to the one owned by Roman Abramovich, though there was no indication the two men knew one another. Abramovich's Chelsea continued to prosper; no oil-fed angel came to Notts County's rescue as they struggled against relegation.

Lynn began to wonder if a sideways move into the National Crime Squad might help to refocus her career.

Resnick saw Eileen one more time. Although most of the money belonging to the man she knew as Michael Sandler had been confiscated, she had inherited enough for new clothes and an expensive makeover, new suitcases which were waiting in the taxi parked outside.

"I thought I'd travel, Charlie. See the world. Switzerland, maybe. Fly round some mountains." Her smile was near to perfect. "You know the only place I've been abroad? If you don't count the Isle of Man. Alicante. Apart from the heat, it wasn't like being abroad at all. Even the announcements in the supermarket were in English."

"Enjoy it," Resnick said. "Have a good time."

Eileen laughed. "Come with me, why don't you? Chuck it all in. About time you retired."

"Thanks a lot."

For a moment her face went serious. "You think we could ever have got together, Charlie?"

"In another life, maybe."

"Which life is that?"

Resnick smiled. "The one where I'm ten years younger and half a stone lighter; not already living with somebody else."

"And not a policeman?"

"Maybe that too."

Craning upwards, she kissed him quickly on the lips. "You're a good man, Charlie, and don't let anyone tell you otherwise."

Long after she had gone, he could feel the pressure of her

mouth on his and smell the scent of her skin beneath the new perfume.

§ § §

For K.C. Constantine, with gratitude and admiration, in particular for his marvellous novel, "Blood Mud", from which the salad finger episode is stolen.

Well, You Needn't

November the third, ninety-four, and it was Resnick's birthday. He just wasn't saying which one. Two days more and he would have been celebrating alongside scores of others, fireworks and bonfires, the burns unit at Queen's Medical on full alert and the Fire Service stretched to near-breaking. As it was, he treated himself to a rare cooked breakfast, eggs and ham and some left-over potatoes fried to the point of crispness, two mugs of coffee instead of the usual one. The cats hovered around his feet, hoping for titbits of rind.

Outside, it was as cold as Margaret Thatcher's heart.

Ten years since she had broken the miners; broken them with the help, if not of Resnick himself then men like him. Her Majesty's Constabulary. Even now, Resnick shrivelled at the thought.

He had a pal, Peter Waites, who had stood shoulder to shoulder on the picket line until he was clubbed to the ground. Still lived in the same two-up, two-down Coal Board house in Arkwright Town. Ten years on the dole. When his son, Jack, had joined the Force as a young PC, Peter Waites had buckled with the shame.

"It's not coppers as is the enemy," Jack had said. "They're just takin' orders, same as everyone else."

Waites had stared away, remembering the clash and clatter of horses' hoofs on cobbled streets, the flare of pain as the truncheon struck his shoulder blade, chipping bone.

Now his lad was attached to CID and stationed at Canning Circus under Resnick's command.

"Congratulations in order, I hear," Millington said, greeting Resnick at the top of the stairs. "Another year closer to retirement." A smile hovered furtively beneath the edges of his moustache. "Be drinks all round tonight, I dare say. Bit of a celebration."

Resnick grunted and carried on past: inside his office he firmly closed the door. When it opened again, some forty minutes later, it was Jack Waites, notebook in hand.

"Come in, lad," Resnick said. "Take a seat."

Waites preferred to stand.

"How's your dad?

"Bitter. Bloody-minded. Same as bloody ever." The young man had held his gaze.

"What can I do for you?" Resnick asked.

"That break-in at the Green Man. Looks like it was Shotter right enough. Prints all over't window frame in back."

Resnick sighed. Three nights before someone had broken into the rear of a pub off the Alfreton Road and made off with a small haul of spirits and cigarettes, the petty cash from the till.

Like Jack Waites' father, Barrie Shotter's life had been shattered by the Miners' Strike: in common with many in the Nottinghamshire pits, he had ignored the strike call and continued to report for work. The windows of his house were smashed. SCAB in foot-high paint on his walls and scratched into his front door. Wife and kiddies jostled in the streets. One morning a group of flying pickets overturned his car; stones were thrown and a sliver of glass spooned out his right eye like the yolk of a boiled egg, neat and entire.

For months he sat in a darkened room and drank: drank away the rent money and the furniture and what little bit they'd saved. When his wife borrowed the bus fare and took the kids back to her mum's in Derby, he tried to hang himself but failed. Took to thieving instead. He was already on probation following his last offence: prison this time, without fail.

Waites was eager to pick him up, make an arrest.

"Later," Resnick said wearily. "Later. He's not going anywhere."

That morning Resnick had a meeting scheduled with the Assistant Chief Constable, himself and a dozen other officers of similar rank — strategy, long-term goals, deference and long words. On the way back he dropped into a record shop on one of the arcades between Upper Parliament Street and Angel Row. Mostly CDs now, of course, but still some racks of vinyl, second-hand. A double album with a slightly dog-eared cover caught his eye: *Thelonious Monk Live at the Jazz Workshop*. The titles were mostly tunes he recognised. "Round Midnight". "Misterioso". "Blue Monk". Recorded in San Francisco over two nights in 1964. November 3rd and 4th. Resnick smiled and reached for his wallet: what better gift?

Barrie Shotter lived in the Meadows, a terraced house not so far from the recreation ground. Jack Waites and two other officers had presented the warrant at the door, Resnick hanging back. Now while they searched the upstairs, cock-a-hoop over finding bottles of vodka and scotch, Bensons King Size by the score, Resnick sat across from Shotter in the small kitchen, neither man speaking, the kettle boiling away behind them, ignored.

There were pictures of Shotter's children, three boys and a girl, all under ten, thumbtacked to the cupboard by the stove.

Spotted now and splashed with grease.

Resnick made tea while his men made an inventory.

Shotter mumbled thanks, stirred in two spoons of sugar and then a third.

"You're a daft bugger, Barrie," Resnick said.

"Tell me something I don't know," Shotter said.

They took him away and double locked the door.

There was a wedge of bread pudding waiting on his desk with a candle sticking out of it, Millington's idea of a joke. He stood the troops a couple of rounds in the pub across the street, put fifty pounds behind the bar and left them to it.

At home he fed the cats then made himself a sandwich, toasted cheese. A shot of whisky in a water glass. His birthday present to himself was on the stereo. A jinking upturned phrase from Monk's piano, the same repeated twice, three times, before the advent of bass and drums and then the saxophone. "Well, You Needn't", November 3rd.

Resnick leaned back in the chair to listen and when the smallest of the cats jumped up onto his lap he let it stay.

Home

Resnick was unable to sleep. All those years of living alone, just the weight of the cats, one and occasionally more, pressing lightly down on the covers by his feet or in the V behind his legs, and now, with Lynn away for just forty-eight hours, he was lost without her by his side. The warmth of her body next to his, the small collisions as they turned from their respective dreams into a splay of legs, her arm sliding across his chest. "Lay still, Charlie. Another five minutes, okay?" Musk of her early morning breath.

He pushed away the sheet and swivelled round, then rose to his feet. Through an inch of open window, he could hear the slight swish of cars along the Woodborough Road. Not so many minutes short of two a.m.

Downstairs, Dizzy, the oldest of the four cats, a warrior no longer, raised his head from the fruit bowl he had long since appropriated as a bed, cocked a chewed and half-torn ear and regarded Resnick with a yellow eye.

Padding past, Resnick set the kettle to boil and slid a tin of coffee beans from the fridge. A flier announcing Lynn's course was pinned to the cork board on the wall — *Unzipping the Agenda: A Guide to Creative Management and Open Thinking*. Lynn and forty or so other officers from the East Midlands and East

Anglia at a conference centre and hotel beside the A1 outside Stevenage. Promotion material. High fliers. When she had joined the Serious Crime Unit barely two years ago, it has been as a sergeant; an inspector now and barely thirty, unless somehow she blotted her copy book, the only way was up. Whereas for Resnick, who had turned down promotion and the chance to move onto a bigger stage, little more than a pension awaited once his years were in.

While the coffee dripped slowly through its filter, Resnick opened the back door into the garden and, as he did so, another of the cats, Pepper, slithered past his ankles. Beyond the allotments, the lights of the city burned dully through a haze of rain and mist. Down there, on the streets of St. Ann's and the Meadows, armed officers patrolled with Walther P990s holstered at their hips. Drugs, of course, the cause of most of it, the cause and the core: all the way from after-dinner cocaine served at trendy middle-class dinner parties alongside the squares of Green and Black's dark organic chocolate, to twenty-five pound wraps of brown changing hands in the stairwells of dilapidated blocks of flats.

Bolting the door, he carried his coffee through into the living room, switched on the light and slid a CD into the stereo. *Art Pepper Meets the Rhythm Section*, Los Angeles, January 19th, 1957. Pepper only months out of jail on drugs offences, his second term and still only thirty-two. And worse to come.

Resnick had seen him play in Leicester on the British leg of his European tour; Pepper older, wiser, allegedly straightened out, soon to be dead three years shy of sixty, a small miracle that he survived that long. That evening, in the function room of a nondescript pub, his playing had been melodic and inventive, the tone piping and lean, its intensity controlled. Man earning a living, doing what he can.

Back in fifty-seven, in front of Miles Davis's rhythm section, he had glittered, half-afraid, inspired, alto saxophone dancing over the chords of half-remembered tunes. "Star Eyes", "Imagination," "Jazz Me Blues". The track that Resnick would play again and again: "You'd Be So Nice To Come Home To".

For a moment Pepper's namesake cat appeared in the doorway, sniffed the air and turned away, presenting his fine tail.

Just time for Resnick, eyes closed, to conjure up a picture of Lynn, restlessly sleeping in a strange bed, before the phone began to ring.

It was the sergeant on duty, his voice stretched by tiredness: "...ten, fifteen minutes ago, sir. I thought you'd want to know."

That stretch of the Ilkeston Road was a mixture of small shops and residential housing, old factories put to new use, student accommodation. Police cars were parked, half on the kerb, either side of a black Ford Mondeo that, seemingly, had swerved wildly and collided, broadside-on, into a concrete post, amidst a welter of torn metal and splintered glass. Onlookers, some with overcoats pulled over their night clothes and carpet slippers on their feet, stood back behind hastily strung-out police tape, craning their necks. An ambulance and fire engine stood opposite, paramedics and fire officers mingling with uniformed police at the perimeter of the scene. Lights flashing, a second ambulance was pulling away as Resnick arrived.

Driving slowly past, he stopped outside a shop, long boarded-up, *High Class Butcher* in faded lettering on the brick-work above.

Anil Khan, once a DC in Resnick's squad and now a sergeant with Serious Crime, came briskly down to meet him and walked him back.

"One dead at the scene, sir, young female; one on his way to hospital, the driver. Female passenger, front near side, her leg's trapped against the door where it buckled in. Have to be cut out most likely. Oxyacetylene."

Resnick could see the body now, stretched out against the lee of the wall beneath a dark grey blanket that was darker at the head.

"Impact?" Resnick said. "Thrown forward against the windscreen?"

Khan shook his head. "Shot."

It stopped Resnick in his tracks.

"Another car, as best we can tell. Three shots, maybe four. One of them hit her in the neck. Must have nicked an artery. She was dead before we got her out."

Illuminated by the street light above, Resnick could see the blood, sticky and bright, clinging to the upholstery like a second skin. Bending towards the body, he lifted back the blanket edge and looked down into the dead startled eyes of a girl of no more than sixteen.

Fifteen years and seven months. Alicia Ann Faye. She had lived with her mother, two younger sisters and an older brother in Radford. A bright and popular student, a lovely girl. She had been to an eighteenth birthday party with her brother, Bradford, and his girl friend, Marlee. Bradford driving.

They had been on their way home when the incident occurred, less than half a mile from where Alicia and Bradford lived. A blue BMW drew up alongside them at the lights before the turn into Ilkeston Road, revving its engine as if intent on racing. Anticipating the green, Bradford, responding to the challenge, accelerated downhill, the BMW in close pursuit; between the first set of lights and the old Radford Mill building, the BMW drew alongside, someone lowered the rear window, pushed a handgun through and fired four times. One shot ricocheted off the roof, another embedded itself in the rear of the front seat; one entered the fleshy part of Bradford's shoulder, causing him to swerve; the fourth and fatal shot struck

Alicia low in side of the neck and exited close to her windpipe.

An impulse shooting, is that what this was? Or a case of mistaken identity?

In the October of the previous year a gunman had opened fire from a passing car, seemingly at random, into a group of young people on their way home from Goose Fair, and a fourteen-year-old girl had died. There were stories of gun gangs and blood feuds in the media, of areas of the inner city running out of control, turf wars over drugs. Flowers and sermons, blame and recriminations and in the heart of the city a minute's silence, many people wearing the dead girl's favourite colours; thousands lined the streets for the funeral, heads bowed in respect.

Now this.

Understaffed as they were, low on morale and resources, policing the city, Resnick knew, was becoming harder and harder. In the past eighteen months, violent crime had risen to double the national average; shootings had increased fourfold. In Radford, Jamaican Yardies controlled the trade in heroin and crack cocaine, while on the Bestwood estate, to the north, the mainly white criminal fraternity was forging an uneasy alliance with the Yardies, all the while fighting amongst themselves; at either side of the city centre, multi-racial gangs from St. Ann's and The Meadows, Asian and Afro-Caribbean, fought out a constant battle for trade and respect.

So was Alicia simply another victim in the wrong place at the wrong time? Or something more? The search for the car was on: best chance it would be found on waste land, torched; ballistics were analysing the bullets from the scene; Bradford Faye and his family were being checked through records; friends would be questioned, neighbours. The public relations department had prepared a statement for the media, another for the Assistant Chief Constable. Resnick sat in the CID office in

Canning Circus station with Anil Khan and Detective Inspector Maureen Price from Serious Crime. His patch, their concern. Their case more than his.

Outside the sky had lightened a little, but still their reflections as they sat were sharp against the window's plate glass.

Maureen Price was in her early forties, no nonsense, matter-of-fact, wearing loose-fitting grey trousers, a zip-up jacket, hair tied back. "So what do we think? We think they were targeted or what?"

"The girl?"

"No, not the girl."

"The brother, then?"

"That's what I'm thinking." The computer print-out was in her hand. "He was put under a supervision order a little over two years back, offering to supply a class A drug."

"That's when he'd be what?" Khan asked "Fifteen?"

"Sixteen. Just."

"Anything since?"

"Not according to this."

"You think he could still be involved?" Resnick said.

"I think it's possible, don't you?"

"And this was what? Some kind of pay-back?"

"Pay-back, warning, who knows? Maybe he was trying to step up into a different league, change his supplier, hold back his share of the cut, anything."

"We've checked with the Drug Squad that he's a player?" Resnick asked.

Maureen Price looked over at Khan, who shook his head. "Haven't been able to raise anyone so far."

The detective inspector looked at her watch. "Try again. Keep trying."

Freeing his mobile from his pocket, Khan walked towards the far side of the room.

"How soon can we talk to Bradford, I wonder?" Resnick said.

"He's most likely still in surgery now. Mid-morning, I'd say. The earliest."

"You want me to do that?"

"No, it's okay. I've asked them to call me from Queen's the minute he's out of recovery. There's an officer standing by." She moved from the desk where she'd been sitting, stretching out her arms and breathing in stale air. "Maybe you could talk to the family?" She smiled. "They're on your patch, Charlie, after all."

There were bunches of flowers already tied to the post into which the car had crashed, some anonymous, some bearing hastily written words of sympathy. More flowers rested up against the low wall outside the house. The victim support officer met Resnick at the door.

"How they holding up?" he asked.

"Good as can be expected, sir."

Resnick nodded and followed the officer into a narrow hall.

"They're in back."

Clarice Faye sat on a green high-backed settee, her youngest daughter cuddled up against her, face pressed to her mother's chest. The middle daughter, Jade, twelve or thirteen, sat close but not touching, head turned away. Clarice was slender, light-skinned, lighter than her daughters, shadows scored deep beneath her eyes. Resnick was reminded of a woman at sea, stubbornly holding on against the pitch and swell of the tide.

The room itself was neat and small, knick-knacks and framed photographs of the children, uniform smiles; a crucifix, metal on a wooden base, hung above the fireplace. The curtains, a heavy stripe, were still pulled part-way across.

Resnick introduced himself and expressed his sympathy; accepted the chair that was offered, narrow with wooden arms, almost too narrow for his size.

"Bradford — have you heard from the hospital?"

"I saw my son this morning. He was sleeping. They told me to come home and get some rest." She shook her head and squeezed her daughter's hand tight. "As if I could."

"He'll be all right?"

"He will live."

The youngest child began to cry.

"He is a good boy, Bradford. Not wild. Not like some. Not any more. Why would anyone...?" She stopped to sniff away a tear. "He is going to join the army, you know that? Has been for an interview already, filled in the forms." She pulled a tissue, screwed and damp, from her sleeve. "A man now, you know? He makes me proud."

Resnick's eyes ran round the photographs in the room. "Alicia's father," he ventured, "is he...?"

"He doesn't live with us any more."

"But he's been told?"

"You think he cares?"

The older girl sprang to her feet and half-ran across the room.

"Jade, come back here."

The door slammed hard against the frame.

Resnick leaned forward, drew his breath. "Bradford and Alicia, last night, you know where they'd been?"

"The Meadows. A friend of Bradford's, his eighteenth."

"Did they often go around together like that, Bradford and Alicia?"

"Sometimes, yes."

"They were close then?"

"Of course." An insult if it were otherwise, a slight.

"And his girlfriend, she didn't mind?"

"Marlee, no. She and Alicia, they were like mates. Pals."

"Mum," the younger girl said, raising her head. "Licia didn't like her. Marlee. She didn't."

"That's not so."

"It is. She told me. She said she smelled."

"Nonsense, child." Clarice smiled indulgently and shook her head.

"How about Alicia?" Resnick asked. "Did she have any boyfriends? Anyone special?"

The hesitation was perhaps a second too long. "No. She was a serious girl. Serious about her studies. She didn't have time for that sort of thing. Besides, she was too young."

"She was sixteen."

"Too young for anything serious, that's what I mean."

"But parties, like yesterday, that was okay?"

"Young people together, having fun. Besides, she had her brother to look after her…"

Tears rushed to her face and she brushed them aside.

The phone rang and the victim support officer answered it in the hall. "It's Bradford," he said from the doorway. "They'll be taking him back up to the ward any time."

"Quickly," Clarice said to her daughter, bustling her off the settee. "Coat and shoes."

Resnick followed them out into the hall. Door open, Jade was sitting on one of the beds in the room she and Alicia had obviously shared. Aware that Resnick was looking at her, she swung her head sharply towards him, staring hard until he moved away.

Outside, clouds slid past in shades of grey; on the opposite side of the narrow street, a couple slowed as they walked by. Resnick waited while the family climbed into the support officer's car and drove away. … *a good boy, Bradford. Not wild. Not any more.* The crucifix. The mother's words. Amazing, he thought, how we believe what we want to believe, all evidence aside.

On the Ilkeston Road, he stopped and crossed the street. There were more flowers now, and photographs of Alicia, covered in plastic against the coming rain. A large teddy bear with black ribbon in a bow around its neck. A dozen red roses wrapped in cellophane, the kind on sale in garage forecourts. Resnick stooped and looked at the card. *For Alicia. Our love will live forever. Michael.* Kisses, drawn in red biro in the shape of a heart, surrounded the words.

Resnick was putting the last touches of a salad together when he heard Lynn's key in the lock. A sauce of spicy sausage and tomato was simmering on the stove; a pan of gently bubbling water ready to receive the pasta.

"Hope you're good and hungry."

"You know…" Her head appearing round the door. "…I'm not sure if I am."

But she managed a good helping nonetheless, wiping the spare sauce from her plate with bread, washing it down with wine.

"So — how was it?" Resnick asked between mouthfuls.

"All right, I suppose."

"Not brilliant then."

"No, some of it was okay. Useful even."

"Such as?"

"Oh, ways of avoiding tunnel vision. Stuff like that."

Resnick poured more wine.

"I just wish," Lynn said, "they wouldn't get you to play these stupid games."

"Games?"

"You know, if you were a vegetable, what vegetable would you be? If you were a car, what car?"

Resnick laughed. "And what were you?"

"Vegetable or car?"

"Either."

"A first crop potato, fresh out of the ground."

"A bit mundane."

"Come on, Charlie, born and brought up in Norfolk, what do you expect?"

"A turnip?"

She waited till he was looking at his plate, then clipped him round the head.

Later, in bed, when he pressed against her back and she turned inside his arms, her face close to his, she said: "Better watch out, Charlie, I didn't tell you what kind of car."

"Something moderately stylish, compact, not too fast?"

"A Maserati Coupé 4.2 in Azuro Blue with full cream leather upholstery."

He was still laughing when she stopped his mouth with hers.

The bullet that had struck Bradford's shoulder was a 9mm, most likely from a plastic Glock. Patched up, replenished with blood, Bradford was sore, sullen, and little else. Aside from lucky. His girlfriend, Marlee, had twenty-seven stitches in a gash in her leg, several butterfly stitches to one side of her head and face and bruises galore. The BMW was found on open ground near railway tracks on the far side of Sneinton, burned out. No prints, no ejected shell cases, nothing of use. It took the best part of a week, but thirty-seven of the fifty or so people who had been at the party in The Meadows were traced, tracked down and questioned. For officers, rare and welcome overtime.

The Drug Squad had no recent information to suggest that Bradford was, again, dealing drugs, but there were several people at the party well known to them indeed. Troy James and Jason Fontaine in particular. Both had long been suspected of playing an active part in the trade in crack cocaine: suspected, arrested, interrogated, charged. James had served eighteen months of a three year sentence before being released; Fontaine had been charged with possession of three kilos of amphetamine with intent to supply, but due to alleged contamination of evidence, the case against him had been dismissed. More recently, the pair of them had been suspected of breaking into a chemist's shop in Wilford and stealing several cases of cold remedies in order to manufacture crystal meth.

James and Fontaine were questioned in the street, questioned in their homes; brought into the police station and questioned again. Bradford spent as much as fourteen hours, broken over a number of sessions, talking to Maureen Price and Anil Khan.

Did he know Troy James and Jason Fontaine?

No.

He didn't know them?

No, not really.

Not really?

Not, you know, to talk to.

But they were at the party.

If you say so.

Well, they were there. James and Fontaine.

Okay, so they were there. So what?

You and Fontaine, you had a conversation.

What conversation?

There are witnesses, claim to have seen you and Fontaine in conversation.

A few words, maybe. I don't remember.

A few words concerning…?

Nothing important. Nothing.

How about an argument … a bit of pushing and shoving?

At the party?

At the party.

No.

Think. Think again. Take your time. It's easy to get confused.

Oh, that. Yeah. It was nothing, right? Someone's drink got spilled, knocked over. Happens all the time.

That's what it was about? The argument?

Yeah.

A few punches thrown?

Maybe.

By you?

Not by me.

By Fontaine?

Fontaine?

Yes. You and Fontaine, squaring up to one another

No. No way.

"There's something there, Charlie," Maureen Price said. "Something between Bradford and Jason Fontaine."

They were sitting in the Polish Diner on Derby Road, blueberry pancakes and coffee, Resnick's treat.

"Something personal?"

"To do with drugs, has to be. Best guess, Fontaine and Ford were using Bradford further down the chain and some way he held out on them, cut the stuff again with glucose, whatever. Either that, or he was trying to branch out on his own, their patch. Radford kid poaching in The Meadows, we all know how that goes down."

"You'll keep on at him?"

"The girlfriend, too. She's pretty shaken up still. What happened to Alicia. Keeps thinking it could have been her, I shouldn't wonder. Flakey as anything. One of them'll break sooner or later."

"You seem certain."

Maureen paused, fork halfway to her mouth. "It's all we've got, Charlie."

Resnick nodded and reached for the maple syrup: maybe just a little touch more.

The flowers were wilting, starting to fade. One or two of the brighter bunches had been stolen. Rain had seeped down into plastic and cellophane, rendering the writing for the most part illegible.

Clarice Faye came to the door in a dark housecoat, belted tight across; there were shadows still around her eyes.

"I'm sorry to disturb you," Resnick said.

A slight shake of the head: no move to invite him in.

"When we were talking before, you said Alicia didn't have any boyfriends, nobody special?"

"That's right."

"Not Troy James?"

"I don't know that name?"

"How about Jason? Jason Fontaine?

The truth was there on her face, a small nerve twitching at the corner of her eye.

"She did go out with Jason Fontaine?"

"She saw him once or twice. The end of last year. He came round here in his car, calling for her. I told him, he wasn't suitable, not for her. Not for Alicia. He didn't bother her again."

"And Alicia…?"

"Alicia understood." Clarice stepped back and began to close the door. "If you'll excuse me now?"

"How about Michael?" Resnick said.

"I don't know no Michael."

And the door closed quietly in his face.

He waited until Jade was on her way home from school, white shirt hanging out, coat open, skirt rolled high over dark tights, clumpy shoes. Her and three friends, loud across the pavement, one of them smoking a cigarette.

None of the others as much as noticed Resnick, gave him any heed.

"I won't keep you a minute," Resnick said as Jade stopped, the others walking on, pace slowed, heads turned.

"Yeah, right."

"You and Alicia, you shared a room."

"So."

"Secrets."

"What secrets?"

"Jason Fontaine, was she seeing him any more?"

Jade tilted back her head, looked him in the eye. "He was just a flash bastard, weren't he? Didn't care nothin' for her."

"And Michael?"

"What about him?"

"You tell me."

"He loved her, didn't he?"

Michael Draper was upstairs in his room: computer, stereo, books and folders from the course he was taking at City College, photographs of Alicia on the wall, Alicia and himself somewhere that might have been the Arboretum, on a bench in front of some trees, an old wall, Michael's skin alongside hers so white it seemed to bleed into the photo's edge.

"She was going to tell them, her mum and that, after her birthday. We were going to get engaged."

"I'm sorry."

The boy's eyes empty and raw from tears.

Maureen Price was out of the office, her mobile switched off. Khan wasn't sure where she was.

"Ask her to call me when she gets a chance," Resnick said. "She can get me at home."

At home he made sure the chicken pieces had finished

defrosting in the fridge, chopped parsley, squashed garlic cloves flat, opened a bottle of wine, saw to the cats, flicked through the pages of the *Post*, Alicia's murder now page four. Art Pepper again, turned up loud. Lynn was late, no later than usual, rushed, smiling, weary, a brush of lips against his cheek.

"I need a shower, Charlie, before anything else."

"I'll get this started." Knifing butter into the pan.

It cost Bradford a hundred and fifteen, talked down from one twenty-five. A Brocock ME38 Magnum air pistol converted to fire live ammunition. .22 shells. Standing there at the edge of the car park, shadowed, he smiled: an eye for an eye. Fontaine's motor, his new one, another Beamer, was no more than thirty metres away, close to the light. He rubbed his hands and moved his feet against the cold, the rain that rattled against the hood of his parka, misted his eyes. Another fifteen minutes, no more, he'd be back out again, Fontaine, on with his rounds.

Less that fifteen, it was closer to ten.

Fontaine appeared at the side door of the pub, calling out to someone inside before raising a hand and turning away.

Bradford tensed, smelling his own stink, his own fear; waited until Fontaine had reached towards the handle of the car door, back turned.

"Wait," Bradford said, stepping out of the dark.

Seeing him, seeing the pistol, Fontaine smiled. "Bradford, my man."

"Bastard," Bradford said, moving closer. "You killed my sister."

"That slag!" Fontaine laughed. "Down on her knees in front of any white meat she could find."

Hands suddenly sticky, slick with sweat despite the cold, Bradford raised the gun and fired. The first shot missed, the second shattered the side window of the car, the third took

Fontaine in the face splintering his jaw. Standing over him, Bradford fired twice more into his body as it slumped towards the ground, then ran.

After watching the news headlines, they decided on an early night. Lynn washed the dishes left over from dinner, while Resnick stacked away. He was locking the door when the phone went and Lynn picked it up. Ten twenty-three.

"Charlie," she said, holding out the receiver. "It's for you."

What Would You Say?

What would you say of a man who can play
three instruments at once — saxophone,
manzello and stritch — but who can neither
tie his shoelace nor button his fly?

Who stumbles through basements,
fumbles open lacquered boxes, a child's set of drawers,
strews their contents across bare boards —
seeds, vestments, rabbit paws?

Whose favourite words are "vertiginous".
"gourd", "dilate"? Whose fantasy is snow?
Who can trace in the dirt the articular process
of the spine, the pulmonary action of the heart?

Would you say he was blind?

Would you say he was missing you?

Ghost of a Chance

He plays the tune lazily,
pretty much the way he must
have heard Billie sing it,
but slower, thick-toned,
leaning back upon the beat,
his mind half on the melody,
half on the gin.

Between takes he stands,
head down, shrunken inside
a suit already overlarge,
cheeks sunken in.
He thinks of her, Billie
already it is possible
he has started to bleed within.

From the control room, laughter,
but that's not what he hears;
tenor closer to his mouth
he turns towards the doors:
unseen, not quite unbidden,
someone has just slipped in.

At the end of eight bars
he closes his eyes and blows.
After two choruses he will cover
his mouthpiece with its shield:
not play again.

Chet Baker

looks out from his hotel room
across the Amstel to the girl
cycling by the canal who lifts
her hand and waves and when
she smiles he is back in times
when every Hollywood producer
wanted to turn his life
into that bittersweet story
where he falls badly, but only
in love with Pier Angeli,
Carol Lynley, Natalie Wood;
that day he strolled into the studio,
fall of fifty-two, and played
those perfect lines across
the chords of My Funny Valentine —
and now, when he looks up from
his window and her passing smile
into the blue of a perfect sky,
he knows this is one of those
rare days when he can truly fly.

Art Pepper

New York, 1972.
The Village Vanguard, Thursday night.
The first of three.

A steady pulse from bass and drums:
the pianist feeds him eight bars
then eight again
and then sixteen.

Faces swim and blur
and still he stands,
alto cradled stillborn
in both hands.

Coke, heroin, methadone,
a gallon of cheap wine a day,
spleen ruptured and removed,
slowly he lifts the mouthpiece
to his lips.

Prison brought him night sweats,
pain, purged him of everything
but this —

The reed like burnt rubber
in his mouth, notes scatter
and break like cinders underfoot.

As long as he can play he lives:
until he dies just five years later
he will remember this.

Saturday

Having slept through
the entire Cup Final
our daughter stumbles
blearily into the room
eyes wild and hair askew
demanding food.

A family of foxes
two adults and three stubby cubs
is living in our garden
littering it with waste and bones.

Frances died, Jim,
after thirty-five years of marriage.
When we were teenagers
you used to call across
the room we shared,
"Good night, John,
and God Bless."

This evening at the Vortex,
shoulder hunched and
greying hair brushed back,
Stan Tracey, well past seventy,
fingers percussive and strong,
played Monk's "Rhythm-a-Ning"
scuttling crab-like across the keys
and I thought of her and you
and all there was between
you. Interlocked.

This then is what we do,
the only thing we can,
sometimes solo,
sometimes hand in hand:
forward, sideways,
sideways, back.

Out of Silence

How the light diffuses round house corners —
Redwood walls, the breaking colour of packed earth,
Ochre in the mouth:
The red woodpecker testily chiselling sap from a small ash
The only sound in the valley.

Acknowledgments

Stories

"Minor Key" was originally published in *Paris Noir*, edited by Maxim Jakubowski, Serpent's Tail, London, 2007

"Billie's Blues" was first published by Éditions Payot & Rivages, Paris, 2002

"The Sun, the Moon and the Stars" first appeared in *The Detection Collection*, edited by Simon Brett, Orion, 2005

"Well, You Needn't" was first published by Otava, Helsinki, 2004

"Home" first appeared in *Ellery Queen Mystery Magazine*, December 2005

Poems

"Ghost of a Chance" & "Chet Baker" were published in *Ghosts of a Chance*, Smith/Doorstop Books, Huddersfield, 1992

"What Would You Say?" & "Out of Silence" were published in *Bluer Than This*, Smith/Doorstop Books, Huddersfield, 1998

"Art Pepper" & "Saturday" are published here for the first time

John Harvey at Five Leaves

Trouble in Mind (Crime Express) — a Resnick novella
Nick's Blues — young adult fiction

Further individual Resnick stories appear in
City of Crime edited by David Belbin
Sunday Night and Monday Morning edited by James Urquhart

John Harvey's poems "Driven by Rain" and "Apples" appear
in *Poetry: the Nottingham Collection* edited by John Lucas

www.fiveleaves.co.uk